Lucy Mastermind

Lucy
Mastermind

by Alan Feldman

illustrated by Irene Trivas

E. P. Dutton   New York

The author and publisher gratefully acknowledge permission to quote on page 94 from *The Iliad of Homer*, translated by Richmond Lattimore, published by the University of Chicago. Copyright 1951 by the University of Chicago. All rights reserved.

Library of Congress Cataloging in Publication Data

Feldman, Alan, date.
    Lucy mastermind.
    Summary: The adventures of Lucy, her friends, and family, at home and at school, as she attempts to restore her family's decrepit boathouse that has a dance floor on the second floor, so that she can have a double birthday party for her mother and her cat.
    [1. Family life—Fiction. 2. Schools—Fiction]
I. Trivas, Irene, ill. II. Title.
PZ7.F33575Lu 1985 [Fic] 85–10094
ISBN 0–525–44155–7

Published in the United States by E. P. Dutton,
2 Park Avenue, New York, N.Y. 10016

Published simultaneously in Canada by
Fitzhenry & Whiteside Limited, Toronto

Editor: Julie Amper   Designer: Isabel Warren-Lynch

Printed in the U.S.A.   W   First Edition
10 9 8 7 6 5 4 3 2 1

for my family—
my wife, Nanette; my son, Daniel;
and, especially, my daughter, Rebecca

Contents

1
The Boathouse

Early in the morning on the first of May, Lucy Heller opened her eyes and knew she would have to hurry. She wanted to get down to the dock before it was time to catch the school bus.   Sam, her five-year-old brother, was still snoring in the bunk underneath hers. It was a comforting, steady sound. She could stretch out here on the top bunk, listen to his noisy sleeping, and imagine Sam was the motor of a ship and she was going somewhere on a voyage. But she had no time for that now.

For breakfast Lucy had a boiled egg with a runny yolk. She ate it quickly, without looking down. Then she jumped up, strapped on her book bag, gave her mother and her father a kiss, and ran out the kitchen door. Lucy knew she was supposed to go straight to the bus stop. But she glanced once over her shoulder to see if anyone was watching her from the window. It was empty, so she scooted down to the boathouse.

On the dock, right next to the boathouse, the gray wooden boards were already warm in the morning sun, and the waves were slapping peacefully against the pilings. Lucy walked to the edge, pulled on a soft laundry-line rope that went down into the water, and brought up her minnow trap. Sure enough, inside the steel basket of the trap, four tiny minnows and two good-sized ones were swimming.

When Lucy brought the trap up into the air, the fish flopped to the bottom of the screening and splashed in a panic. She reached in, picked out each of the tiny minnows by its thin, prickly tail, and threw them back. They swam off like little flakes of gold in the dark green water under the dock. Now she grabbed the larger fish by their tails. These she knew she had to bang against the dock. As soon as she did, they were still.

"Marmalade!" she called. "Marmalade!" She wanted to yell, but she didn't want to yell too loud, or her mother and father might know she'd stopped down here. But the cat heard her. She saw his reddish body dashing through the low bushes that grew beside the lake.

"It's May today," Lucy said to the cat, whose fur was already warm. He must have been sleeping in the sun, she thought as his silky body swept along her arm. "It's May, Marmalade, and it's your birthday today. Your first birthday." Marmalade purred, and rubbed against her. "Here's a present for you," said Lucy. She put the two pale golden fish on the dock in front of Marmalade.

The cat delicately lowered its nose and whiskers to sniff and touch the fish, and Lucy stroked his soft back as he started to eat. Actually Lucy hadn't any idea when Marmalade's birthday was. Sometime in spring, probably, since Marmalade seemed about a year old. And today seemed like the perfect day for him to have his birthday. The weather was so mild.

"Sorry I can't stay with you and watch you eat, but I've got to get to school. In fact, I'll bet Tommy Flint and his bean-pole sister, Betty Jean, are at the bus stop already," Lucy told the cat. "I hope I miss the bus."

Marmalade glanced up at her.

"You're right," said Lucy. "I shouldn't. You're so intelligent, Marmalade. You're a most remarkable creature." That was one of her father's sayings. It was a kind of compliment. Her father admired Marmalade too, though he couldn't touch him or allow him in the house because he was allergic to cat fur.

Well, she really couldn't stay here admiring Marmalade all day. Lucy climbed the steps and started to trudge up the long driveway toward the road. Sure enough, she could see the Flint kids waiting. Tommy was busy trying to hit the light pole across the road with stones. They'd only moved here a week ago, but already Tommy Flint's jeering face had started to look just like a cauliflower to her.

Betty Jean didn't wave. She watched Lucy approaching, and when Lucy reached the road, said, "That's a pretty rickety-looking boathouse you've got down there."

Lucy turned and gave the boathouse a careful look. It was true. It seemed to her that it was tilting even more this spring than it was last fall.

"My dad says nobody should build a boathouse with two stories like that. What's up there on the second floor?"

"A dance floor," said Lucy. "My grandmother and grandfather had it built a long time ago."

"Well, whatever it is, it's going to fall into the lake one of these days."

Maybe, Lucy thought. But she also thought it wasn't very tactful of Betty Jean to have said so. Betty Jean had two long, black braids and big freckles, and right now Lucy wished Betty Jean's freckles would turn into big holes like Swiss cheese. And that the holes would get bigger and bigger and that Betty Jean would disappear. Along with Tommy. Then Lucy could have the bus stop to herself again.

Tommy came scuffling over to where Lucy was standing, and he also began staring down toward the boathouse.

"Is that your cat down on the dock?"

"Not exactly," said Lucy.

"My dog Duke's been hunting for that cat," Tommy said proudly. "And he's going to get him. He's faster than any cat."

Lucy couldn't help being annoyed. "You mean you're telling me you let your dog run around without a leash?" She tried to sound shocked.

"You bet," said Tommy. "And he's hunting for that cat every night. And he's going to get him too."

"Oh, that's a shame," said Lucy. "I'll be forced to report him to the dogcatcher, who'll take him away. Then if the owner doesn't claim him in twelve hours, they put him to sleep. Poor Duke," said Lucy, shaking her head and pretending to be sorry.

Tommy Flint's face seemed to crumple. He looked pleadingly toward his older sister. "You wouldn't report Duke to the dogcatcher, would you?" Betty Jean's voice sounded strangely thin.

"Of course not," said Lucy. "If he doesn't come around my house. And if he doesn't chase Marmalade."

Just then the orange school bus came grinding along the dirt road, raising a cloud of dust. When the bus stopped, Tommy didn't rush to be first on board. Instead both he and Betty Jean let Lucy get on first, so Lucy got to have the one window seat that was left. Neither Tommy nor Betty Jean sat next to her. She wondered if her threat about Duke had worked too well. She hadn't wanted to make them afraid of her. Of course she wouldn't report their stupid big old dog. Besides, the dogcatcher didn't put the dogs to sleep when he had to come and catch them. Not if they had a collar and a tag. And Duke had those.

No, it was just a good story that she had decided might work. And it did. She was sure they'd try to keep their dog away from Marmalade. But now she was already working on a better idea. It had to do with the boathouse that Betty Jean had said was so rickety. In a way Betty Jean was right. A boathouse with a dance floor on top certainly deserved to be kept in better shape. After all, how many boathouses in the whole world had dance floors on top? Why, a dance floor was the nicest, oddest thing a boathouse could possibly have on its second floor—if it had a second floor.

Lucy started to dream about a party on top of the boathouse. Her mother's birthday was coming up, so it could be a double birthday party. For her mother and for Marmalade. With dancing and everything. Lucy had just finished imagining the dress her mother would wear to the party—the green crêpe, of course, it was her mother's favorite—when the school bus pulled in front of the Star Lake Center School and she saw her teacher, Mr. Fallsworth, pacing back and forth on the sidewalk.

2

Electric Motors
and Eskimos

"Hi, Carrot Top!" Mr. Fallsworth called to Lucy. She didn't mind. It was his way of telling her that he was glad to see her. Also, she knew he admired her hair, which came down below her shoulders and was red and wavy. But she wished he'd think of a new nickname occasionally, instead of using the same one all the time. Something like Firefly. Or Tomato Sauce. Or Red-hot Mama. Or any of the other thousands of silly names she could think of to call herself.

In her classroom, Lucy's table was near the window. Lucy liked this. During reading, a patch of sunlight fell on her section of the table, and the words in her books seemed to blaze up off the page, they were so bright. And during math, which always came after reading, she could look out the window in between each problem.

While the class did problem after problem, Lucy did one and then looked out the window. Outside, in the school yard, she could see the maple tree with its baby leaves. They were all scrunched up now, but soon they would be full and green.

"All right, kids! A few more minutes," said Mr. Fallsworth.

Oh dear, thought Lucy. At least half the spaces on her arithmetic page were blank. Hmmm, if a man bought fourteen pairs of boots at $2.99, how much would he spend in all? Lucy read the problem and started to think about the man buying all those boots. He must have a very large family, she thought to herself. Suddenly she remembered feeding Marmalade his breakfast this morning on the dock, and she wished she were with him. She could see him so clearly! Now he was looking at her sympathetically, as if about to tell her the answer. "One plus one," he said, "equals six!"

"Lucy!" Mr. Fallsworth was saying very loudly. "This paper isn't finished. What were you doing with yourself all this time?" She knew from the tone of his voice that she must have done something wrong. But she couldn't very well say to him that her cat had been helping her do arithmetic.

Lucy looked across all the tables, up toward the front of the room where Mr. Fallsworth was sitting behind his desk. His face seemed very red to her. All over. She guessed he was angry at her again. Lucy had a funny feeling in her throat, as if she had swallowed a toothbrush. Or was trying to swallow it but couldn't quite get it down.

"Lucy, my dear," said Mr. Fallsworth, as though he were struggling not to yell at her. "You didn't have your homework this morning. And now you haven't finished even half of the arithmetic. What am I going to do with you?"

The rest of the class was quiet. Lucy didn't think it was fair. They were noisy enough most of the time, but when someone got into trouble, they all were very, very quiet, just to see what awful thing would happen.

Lucy tried hard to think of something Mr. Fallsworth could do with her. She thought he might try forgetting about the whole thing. There was sure to be more arithmetic next week. She would do it next week. Maybe she should promise Mr. Fallsworth that. For a moment Lucy found herself feeling very sorry for Mr. Fallsworth. He seemed so upset, and he didn't know what to do with her. And Lucy didn't know either.

"Maybe you could keep me inside at lunchtime," Lucy suggested.

"Not again," Bobby Lattimore called out, and the rest of the class tittered.

"All right," said Mr. Fallsworth with a sigh. "Stay in at lunchtime."

"Thank you," said Lucy. And this made the class laugh even louder.

But of course, staying inside wasn't a punishment for Lucy. After she made up her work, she could almost always find something interesting to do. Today the Electric Motor Club was meeting in Mr. Fallsworth's room at lunchtime, and Lucy was very curious to see what they were up to.

The Electric Motor Club didn't know much about electric motors. While she worked on row after row of arithmetic problems, a group of kids was sitting at one of the tables across the room. In the middle of the table was an electric motor kit. They were reading the instructions, shouting at each other, and fighting over the tools and the parts. But nobody could get the motor to move when it was hooked up to the battery.

Every once in a while, Mr. Fallsworth would look up from his own desk and give them a suggestion. Emily Minot started to giggle when Bobby Lattimore pulled one of her hair ribbons right out of her hair. Pretty soon the Electric Motor Club members were chasing each other around the room, and Mr. Fallsworth was turning red again and shouting "If you don't want to work on this, then you can all go outside."

The way Mr. Fallsworth said "go outside" made it sound like a punishment. Everyone got quiet. "Here," said Mr. Fallsworth. I'd better give you a hand with this."

The members of the Electric Motor Club clustered around Mr. Fallsworth and watched. Now the parts to the motor were scattered over the table, and Lucy could see that Mr. Fallsworth had to read the instructions himself to know what he was doing. Lucy and her father had built a motor like this at home, and even from where she was sitting, she could see Mr. Fallsworth was going to have trouble. He had the positive lead from the dry-cell battery connected in the wrong place. The back of his neck was burning red as he leaned over the motor.

After a few moments, the children could all see the motor wasn't going to start, and they started getting fidgety and restless again. You had to think about things quietly sometimes, Lucy knew. If you got fidgety, you'd just have to give up.

She wondered if Mr. Fallsworth would let her help. Sometimes people didn't like to be helped. Her brother, Sam, for example. Sometimes Sam liked to be helped in putting his boots on. And sometimes he didn't. Either way, he couldn't do it alone.

Lucy went over to the table.

"Mr. Fallsworth, Lucy's not doing her arithmetic. She's over here with the Electric Motor Club, and she isn't supposed to be," Emily said.

Mr. Fallsworth looked up at Lucy with annoyance. "Did you finish?"

"I just wanted to help you," said Lucy. "These sorts of motors can be very tricky."

"Oh, they can, can they?" said Mr. Fallsworth. He was smiling a little, so Lucy figured he couldn't really be annoyed with her. He was probably just annoyed at the motor because it wouldn't run.

"Yes," said Lucy, grabbing a screwdriver, removing the red wire, wrapping it around another little brass screw, and tightening it. "They can be." Just then the motor began to whir very fast. The Electric Motor Club began to cheer.

"OK. We've done it," said Mr. Fallsworth. "It was just a matter of connecting the positive lead properly, you see."

As the kids trooped out into the sunny yard through the door at the back of the classroom, Lucy had a sinking feeling. Mr. Fallsworth was sitting down on the edge of his desk. Lucy could see the reflection of the playground in his glasses. ". . . that was very fine, the way you helped me with the motor," Mr. Fallsworth was saying.

"I know," said Lucy. She felt bad as soon as she said that. Her mother had taught her to say thank-you when someone paid her a compliment.

"Well, then," said Mr. Fallsworth, "since you know you are so intelligent, why don't you do your homework or your arithmetic problems in school?"

Now it was Lucy's turn to sigh. Did he want to hear the whole story? she wondered.

She knew she'd have to explain everything at once, or she'd never get it all out. She'd have to tell him about Sam and how strange he could be. "Well, you know my little brother, Sam? Well, Sam's afraid of almost everything, Mr. Fallsworth. Wood floors, dogs, ice, vitamin pills, Q-Tips, pullover sweaters, mice, bugs—"

"Lucy," said Mr. Fallsworth. "You can just say 'almost everything.' "

"Well, anyway, of course he doesn't like people yelling at him," said Lucy. "And last night my father yelled at him." The truth was that Sam had forgotten the letter *S*. This was the first letter Sam had

14

been able to learn. Lucy thought it was wrong of her father to yell, but in her opinion, he couldn't help it. He had lost all his patience.

"Now, Sam is afraid of loud noises of any kind," Lucy explained to Mr. Fallsworth. "He doesn't like dogs, lawn mowers, garbage trucks, spattering fried chicken, shrieking teakettles, electric drills, motorboats, fire alarms, vacuum cleaners—"

"Lucy," Mr. Fallsworth interrupted, "you could just say 'noises.'"

"Anyway, Mr. Fallsworth, I decided to get him ready for bed myself. I coaxed him along quietly, and then he wanted a story. So I read to him for about half an hour, and then I tucked him into bed. But the whole thing took so long that there wasn't time for me to do my arithmetic homework."

Mr. Fallsworth just stared at Lucy and didn't say anything. He looked as though he were working on arithmetic problems himself.

"And as for my arithmetic this morning," Lucy went on, "the problems all seemed alike. So I looked out the window to see what the weather was like. And I guess I was thinking about Marmalade and his birthday, and my mother's birthday—which is coming up this month—and the boathouse which is going to fall into the lake, and the dance floor on top of the boathouse, and what a great place for a party that would be, and the dress my mother is going to wear, and what I'm going to give Marmalade for his birthday besides the two fish he got this—"

"Lucy!" shouted Mr. Fallsworth. "No more lists! Please!"

"Sorry," said Lucy.

"Now, what are you talking about? What party? What dance floor?"

So Lucy explained more slowly. She left out some of the details about Marmalade, because she didn't know if Mr. Fallsworth would understand why it was so important to have a birthday party for a wild cat who didn't live in anybody's house and only ate fresh fish.

When Lucy finished her arithmetic and was about to head outside for the little bit of time that remained in the lunch period, Mr. Fallsworth stopped her. He was thinking about something, but she couldn't tell what. "You know, Lucy, that boathouse could be jacked up again, and new pilings could be put under it."

"Oh, I know that," said Lucy. "But my father can't do it. It would take a lot of people and some special jacks."

"Why doesn't he get Dave Seally to do it?" Mr. Fallsworth asked. "Dave's got that sort of equipment. And he does that kind of work all the time."

"I'm not sure," said Lucy. "But I think it would cost too much money. We're not exactly poor, but we've got a very big house, and a garage with room for four cars and a whole apartment on top of it, and then the boathouse. And my father says there just

16

isn't enough money to take care of all of that."

"I see," said Mr. Fallsworth. "But maybe Dave Seally would do it cheaply as a favor."

"I don't think so," said Lucy. She had never heard her father say anything about asking Dave Seally for a favor. She wasn't sure her father even knew him that well.

"But doesn't Hilda Quail work for your family?" asked Mr. Fallsworth.

"Oh yes," said Lucy. That was true enough. In fact she was there every day when Lucy got home from school. She knew, of course, that Hilda went out on dates with Dave Seally. Was that what Mr. Fallsworth was getting at?

"Would Dave Seally help us because we know Hilda?" asked Lucy.

"Why don't you ask her that yourself?" said Mr. Fallsworth.

Lucy thought about it. Maybe it was one of those cases where the woman has the man enchanted. Then he would do anything she asked him to. Including fixing up the boathouse at a very great discount. Well, she would ask Hilda. She made up her mind to have a really clever conversation with Hilda as soon as she got home.

The class came back in from recess, and it was time for social studies. She didn't mind that so much. Her assignment was to read all about the Eskimos. She started imagining hunting whales for Marmalade. She wondered how long it would take a cat to finish off a whale.

17

3

Blunderland

When Lucy came home from school, there seemed to be no way to get away from the smell of Hilda's pies. Lucy put down her book bag and inspected an apple pie that seemed to have an extra lump of crust that needed rounding off. Lucy was just about to break off the lump when Hilda came back into the kitchen and put her hand on Lucy's to stop her. Then she carefully broke off the lump herself and put it directly into Lucy's mouth.

"I have to go to the cold cellar to get some more preserves," said Hilda. "Can I trust you here?"

"No," said Lucy. Actually, Lucy didn't mind going along with Hilda to the cold cellar. It would give her the perfect chance to have her clever conversation. As they walked across the lawn, Lucy asked in an offhand way, "Hilda, you go out on dates with Dave Sealy, right?"

"We see each other," said Hilda cheerfully

enough. "After all, he's my sister's husband's brother."

"Is there a name for that? Like brother-in-law? Or brother-brother-in law? Or something like that?"

"Oh heavens, Lucy. Doesn't anyone ever clean this place?"

"It's not *that* dirty, Hilda."

Hilda stood in the doorway of the cold cellar while Lucy brought the jars of preserves to her. In one corner near the back, where light could hardly reach, some old gardening tools were knitted together with cobwebs.

"I hate cold cellars," said Hilda. "We have them back home. I think it's primitive."

Lucy asked Hilda what *primitive* meant.

"Doing things in a coarse way, without any manners," said Hilda.

"Well, I don't think my grandfather was primitive. I think he liked the idea of using a closet in a hillside for a refrigerator."

"Well, I wouldn't know," Hilda confessed. "They do say he's quite a brilliant man, your grandfather."

"*Who* says that?" Lucy asked. She was always fascinated by the things people said about her grandfather. Now, of course, he was very old. Not sick, exactly. But very frail.

"Well," said Hilda. "Dave says that, for one."

"He does?" Lucy asked, happy that Hilda had returned to the subject of Dave Seally. "Hilda,"

19

Lucy asked. "Does Dave really like you a lot? I mean, is he enchanted with you?"

"Is he *what*?" Hilda asked.

"I mean, would he do anything in his power for you? You know, like when someone's enchanted." Lucy had to admit that Hilda didn't look very enchanting right now. Her curly brown hair hardly showed beneath her kerchief, and on her forehead there was a smudge of dust.

Hilda seemed to have lost all her patience with Lucy. She was looking at her watch. "Where's that brother of yours?"

"His bus probably broke down again," Lucy suggested.

"Maybe," said Hilda. "Every time I'm on the verge of calling the police, that old rattletrap overheats and shows up late, late, late." Hilda seemed a bit overheated herself. Lucy decided she might be better off talking to Dave directly.

"There it is!" said Hilda.

And sure enough, down the driveway came Sam's bus, belching its usual clouds of smoke.

Sam's school was all the way over at Tupper Lake. That was because he wasn't in an ordinary class. Sam was small, but he really was five, and he should have been in kindergarten in her school this year. But instead he had to be in a special class for kids who had trouble learning. Lucy had visited his classroom once, and it was certainly much more fun than

20

hers. Sam's teacher had a whole rack of dress-up clothes that the kids could put on anytime they wanted. She wondered how Mr. Fallsworth would feel about that idea.

Sam was usually asleep by the time he got home. Tony, his driver, would give Sam's schoolbag to Lucy to carry into the house. And then Sam would be given to Hilda or to Lucy's mother, if he came so late that their mother was already home from her office. And Sam would look sleepy and rub his eyes until he got into the kitchen. And then he'd sit bolt upright and say "Juice!" Sam was wild about juice. But if you didn't give it to him right away, he could be a real brat.

But the nice thing about Sam, Lucy decided, was that he wasn't boring. What he *usually* did wasn't what he *always* did. Today he was wide-awake and was insisting that the bus was on fire. Maybe he really believed it. The bus did make an awful lot of smoke. He was talking quite severely, and giving orders to Tony. He wanted Tony to drive the bus into the lake. "It's a fire!" he was shouting. "Get a hose! Drive the truck into the water!"

"Bus?" asked Lucy. "You mean the bus is on fire?"

"Yeeeeeeesss!" Sam shrieked with impatience.

"But why do you need a hose, Sam, if you're going to drive the bus into the lake?" Lucy asked. "Wouldn't the bus get wet from the lake? And if it was already wet, then the fire would go out by itself.

21

See?" When he was grouchy like this, Lucy was always tempted to annoy him by being logical.

"You dummy!" shouted Sam. "This truck is on fire!"

"Bus, you mean, Sam, don't you?" Lucy asked in a pretend-sweet voice, though she was really losing her patience with him.

"Uhhh. Bus!" said Sam. "I mean bus."

"OK, Sam. Whatever you say. I'll get the hose." And then she turned to Tony. "Could I really spray the bus? Me and Sam?" Tony nodded.

While Lucy hosed off the bus—it was the first time she'd gotten to use the hose since last summer—Sam stood back, since he was afraid of water. "Some fireman you'd make!" Lucy said to him, and she was really, really tempted to squirt him with water since he hated it so much.

But she didn't. It was enough fun to spray the bus. Who'd have thought she'd get to use the hose this early in the year?

Lucy sprayed the bus a long time, till all the mud was rinsed off its faded blue paint. The bus looked even older and rustier when it was clean, she decided. She wondered when they'd ever get a new bus. She started to imagine a huge, shiny, brand-new school bus—a real school bus, like the one she rode in every day—coming down the driveway and stopping in front of the house. And Sam, the only kid left on board, would be sitting right behind the driver, in his favorite seat.

That evening, as they sat in the living room by the fire, Mr. Heller started to read to Sam and ask him questions. Lucy knew exactly what would happen. Everything would start out fine, and Sam would even know some of the answers. Then Sam would get tired, and he wouldn't know the answers, and her father would get tired, and he'd start yelling.

Sure enough, it wasn't long before Sam seemed to have forgotten the names of some of the animals. They had been looking at *Noises on the Farm.* " 'This is a pig!' " said Mr. Heller, so loud he was almost shouting. " ' "Oink! Oink!" goes the pig.' "

" 'Quack! Quack!' goes the duck!" said Lucy.

"Be quiet," said Mrs. Heller sternly. "Your father is reading to Sam, not to you." Lucy knew she shouldn't interrupt. But she couldn't stand it when Sam was so slow to answer and her father was so impatient.

"What's this, Sam?" Mr. Heller was asking.

"Uhhh," said Sam, looking at Lucy for sympathy. "Pig."

"Goooood!" said Mr. Heller. "Now what's this?"

"Uhhh," said Sam. Now he was really tired of being asked questions. "Cow!"

"No!" said Mr. Heller. "*That's* not a cow! That's a *horse*! HORSE!"

Lucy could tell her father was about to explode. "Don't get mad at him, Daddy," she said. "He's probably just tired of being asked obvious questions. Wouldn't you be?"

"But why does he say a horse is a cow? He really ought to know the difference by now, shouldn't he? I can't deal with him, Nora. I simply can't deal with him!" Now Mr. Heller was shouting in the direction of Lucy's mother. He threw *Noises on the Farm* down on the floor and slammed the door behind him as he left the room.

Sam was sitting in the corner of the big wing chair by the fire. In that big chair, he looked really small to Lucy. And he was shaking. He really did hate to be yelled at.

"Mom, I'll tell Sam a story and put him to bed all by myself. Okay?"

Mrs. Heller was sitting in the other big wing chair by the fire. But it looked as though she were sitting in a big pile of laundry, since she had taken it in from the line and was sorting it. "That's kind of you, Lucy," said her mother.

Actually Lucy didn't feel she was being kind. She really liked getting Sam ready for bed. They jumped up and down on the mattresses for a while. Then she helped Sam get into his pajamas and brush his teeth. And then she began her story. " 'The Adventures of Lucy and Sam in Blunderland'!" she announced.

"Once upon a time there were two kids who seemed to do absolutely everything wrong, and their names were . . ." Lucy paused.

"Charlie!" shouted Sam. That's what he always said if you let him name something.

"No, not Charlie," Lucy laughed. "These kids were named Lucy and Sam, just like us. And one day Lucy and Sam went down to the boathouse. Their mother and father had said, 'Don't you ever go into that boathouse. It could fall into the water any minute.' But they did anyway. And guess what! They found a little—"

"The boathouse fell down?" Sam asked.

"No, Sam. The boathouse did *not* fall down. It was *falling* down. I mean it was *going* to fall down if nobody fixed it."

"It didn't?"

"No, Sam. Now will you let me get on with the story? Anyway. So, these two kids, Lucy and Sam, went into the boathouse, and they found a little door they had never seen before. And they opened it and they crawled through, and they found themselves . . ." Lucy knew that her story was really a lot like *Alice in Wonderland,* but she figured that wouldn't bother Sam, because he didn't know about that one.

"Now in Blunderland," Lucy explained, "nobody can do anything right. If they have a horse and they want to move it, they pick it up. And when it starts to rain, the men get on the roofs of their houses with umbrellas because they're trying to—"

"What are they doing up there?"

"Sam!" Lucy shouted. She was about to get as angry as her father. "Will you let me finish? They're trying to keep their houses from getting wet. . . ." When the story was finished, Sam went to sleep

26

without complaining. Lucy called her parents in to give Sam a kiss. And they gave her a lot of kisses, too, and told her what a good sister she was.

Lucy decided to go to sleep on the upper bunk in Sam's room. It was cozy. And, as usual, she even liked the sound of Sam's snoring. He sounded as though he were working on being asleep.

But that night she had the strangest dream. She followed Marmalade through the little door in the boathouse and then lost him. Instead she kept seeing another cat. It was as if Marmalade had turned into his own shadow. Or into the opposite of his shadow. Because this other cat was pure white.

4
Fishing

The next morning, Lucy's father had gotten back all his patience. It was hard getting Sam dressed in the morning, because he was usually wet, and his soggy pajamas had to be peeled off him. But Lucy's father was sprinkling powder on Sam's skinny, white, freezing body to make him comfortable and dry, and he had figured out a way to make Sam laugh as he was doing it. He was pretending Sam was a cake.

"Here's some flour for this lovely cake!" Mr. Heller was shouting, rubbing the powder onto Sam's stomach, though some of it sprinkled on the blue rug, and some of it sprinkled into Sam's straight, white-gold hair. Sam was giggling. "And here's a nice blue plate," said Mr. Heller, pretending Sam's dungarees were a plate. "And here's some chocolate frosting for the cake!" said Mr. Heller, picking out a brown shirt for Sam to put on. "And here's some suspenders!" he said, putting on Sam's favorite red suspenders. "A cake with suspenders!

28

Very unusual. You know who'd love that? Mom. We can give you to her for a birthday cake."

"I'm a cake!" shouted Sam, very proud of himself. "I'm a cake with spenders!"

"Yes, and we're going to have to stick thirty-five candles into you, Sam, my boy. One for good luck, you know. Mom always wants one for good luck." Mr. Heller was just fastening Sam's pants and kissing him on the neck, tickling Sam with his bushy beard.

"What should I pretend to be?" asked Lucy.

"You're both cakes," said Mr. Heller. "I'll take this chocolate cake in my arms. And I'll take this big strawberry one like so—" And Lucy got to ride down all three flights of stairs clinging to her father's back.

All in all, it was a wonderful morning. Marmalade was down on the dock as usual, waiting for Lucy to feed him. But there was only one not-so-large minnow in the trap this morning.

Lucy asked her father if she could take the rowboat out by herself and go fishing. The rowboat was dark green and made of steel. So you could stamp on the bottom of it, and it would make a sound like a drum.

Lucy got her worms and her tackle and rowed around the point to the other side of the house where the beach was, and the sandbar. You could see the sandbar easily. The water there turned from dark green or dark blue to yellow. Lucy fished steadily all morning and kept catching sunfish. It was a good spot, all right. By the time she was done, the whole bottom of the boat was covered with small, disclike, shiny fish, spread out all around her feet like a treasure, and she couldn't wait for Marmalade to see them.

When she rounded the point again, she saw Tommy and Betty Jean fishing from the end of their dock. Ever since the lake had thawed, they had been trying to learn to fish. But they were too impatient, always jerking in their lines to see what they'd caught and scaring away the fish.

"Catch anything?" Tommy shouted.

"A few," said Lucy.

"Where?" asked Tommy.

"Oh, around the point." Like most fishermen, she wasn't eager to tell anyone else where the best fishing was.

"That's the funniest boat on the lake," Betty Jean said. "I mean, who would want a boat made out of steel? It's so heavy. My father said they haven't made boats like that in years."

"How many fish did you catch?" asked Tommy.

"Oh, a few."

"I'm going to row out to see if you really caught any," said Tommy. "And if you're lying, I'm going to capsize your boat."

Tommy got into his own boat and rowed toward her. Lucy was tempted simply to row away from him. She knew she could row much faster than he could. But then again, she really was proud of her fish. She might even give him a few for Duke, if he asked her politely.

"Betty Jean! You got to see this!" Tommy was shouting. He was holding on to the side of Lucy's boat and leaning over so he could get a good look at the fish on the bottom. Next Lucy heard a splash. Betty Jean had dived in and was swimming, and soon she too was hanging on to the side of Lucy's boat.

"How did you catch those?" Betty Jean asked.

"I just found a good spot," said Lucy. She was trying not to sound too proud of herself. But it was hard not to feel proud when stuck-up Betty Jean was hanging on to the side of her boat, all goose-bumped and shivering from the cold water, and full of amazement.

"Would you like to climb into my boat?" asked Lucy. "That way you can have a better look at the fish." Betty Jean's lips were turning blue.

"If you'd like, I could row you back to your dock."

"Thanks," said Betty Jean.

Betty Jean seemed so grateful to be rescued and so admiring of Lucy's fish, that she was actually nice for once. And this gave Lucy an idea. She had a little project she needed some help with.

"Then, if you want, you could come over to my house and help me put all these fish in the refrigerator."

"Yeah," said Tommy. "And if you don't have enough room, Betty Jean and I could put some in our refrigerator."

31

"Sure," said Lucy. "And after we finish that, you could help me do some surgery."

"Sure," said Tommy.

"What surgery?" asked Betty Jean.

"Well, it's a new idea I have," said Lucy.

Lucy rowed Betty Jean to the dock and then rowed back to her own dock to show Marmalade all the fish she had caught for him. Now he would really see how much she loved him.

Marmalade was certainly impressed. In fact, he seemed overwhelmed. As Lucy put the fish on the dock, he seemed to sniff each one of them. "You can have *one,* Marmalade, but that's all. I don't want you getting sick."

Lucy picked up one of the largest and offered it to the cat. He took it and rubbed up against her leg a moment. But before she could pat him, he ran off into the woods. He looked very funny with the head and tail of the fish sticking out from the sides of his mouth like a big moustache.

Lucy had to make several trips to the house with the fish.

"Dad," Lucy shouted up the stairs. "Could I put the fish I caught into the refrigerator?"

"Sure, honey." When her father was paying his bills, he always said "Sure, honey" to just about any question.

So Lucy started to wrap the fish in waxed paper the way her father had taught her. Before long,

Tommy and Betty Jean came over and started to help her.

"This is the oldest refrigerator I've ever seen," said Betty Jean. "Ours is much bigger."

"True," said Lucy, "but this one is much colder. Does yours freeze milk?"

"Not exactly," said Tommy.

"Refrigerators aren't supposed to freeze milk," said Betty Jean.

"Look we fit nearly all the fish in!" Lucy pointed out with satisfaction. There were only thirty or forty left. The shelves of the old refrigerator were pretty crowded, however.

In between the orange juice and the American cheese, dozens of fish tails were piled up. On top of last night's meat casserole there was a pile of fish. There were six fish in the butter compartment. The ice cream in the freezer was surrounded by fish. There were fish in the vegetable hydrator, all around the carrots. There were even fish on the small top shelf where the jelly was kept. Lucy was sure she could fit some fish inside the lettuce crisper. Tommy suggested putting one inside the egg carton, which wasn't such a bad idea, Lucy decided, considering it came from Tommy.

When they had finished, Lucy's refrigerator was packed from top to bottom with fish. One hundred and forty-three fish. Fish with eyes that stared at her when she opened the door. It sure was an unusual-looking refrigerator, Lucy decided.

5

Sure, Honey

"Dad," Lucy shouted up the stairs again. "Where's Sam?"

"In his room, I think," Mr. Heller shouted back down.

"Tommy and Betty Jean are here, and we're all going to go up to the attic and do some surgery."

"Sure, honey," said Mr. Heller.

They found Sam driving one of his trucks back and forth across the mattress. He kept making what he probably thought were truck noises. "Brrrrrrr. Brrrrrrr." He looked very bored, Lucy decided to herself.

"Hey, Sam, want to come up to the attic and do some surgery?" Lucy asked, trying to get as much excitement into her voice as she could. She knew Sam wouldn't know what surgery was. But if she sounded excited, he might do it.

"OK. We've got our patient," said Lucy to Tommy and Betty Jean as she led them quietly up the flight of stairs to Sam's room. They peeked in.

"Brrrrrrr. Brrrrrrr."

"What's wrong with him?" asked Betty Jean.

"Nothing," said Lucy. "He's just driving."

"Oh," said Betty Jean. "Then why does he need an operation?"

"Well," said Lucy, "we're going to attempt an alphabet operation. See, Sam doesn't quite know his alphabet yet. Or, well, some days he seems to and some days he doesn't. So we're going to fix that."

"How?" asked Tommy.

"With surgery," said Lucy.

"Oh," said Tommy.

"Betty Jean, you will assist me?" Lucy asked.

"I don't know," said Betty Jean doubtfully. "How will we get him up there?"

"He *may* come willingly," said Lucy. "Then again, he may not."

"How about if we make him some pills out of chocolate?" suggested Tommy.

"Have you got any?" Lucy knew that chocolate pills were exactly the right medicine to lure Sam upstairs. Lately Tommy's face was beginning to seem completely human to her, not a bit like a cauliflower.

"A couple of pieces," Tommy said. He drew out of his pocket some chocolate wrapped in silver foil.

"Oh Sam," said Lucy very sweetly and cajolingly. "Look at the *medicine* we have for you!" She waved the chocolate in front of Sam's face. The motor of his truck cut off immediately.

"Come upstairs then," said Lucy. "And get operated on. These"—she waved her hand at Tommy and Betty Jean—"are my assistants."

Sam followed them up the stairs into the attic.

It was a large attic. All in all there must have been hundreds of trunks and boxes up there filled with her grandfather's old medical equipment. Some of this would be just perfect for doing surgery. Lucy picked out an old-fashioned hypodermic that seemed to be made of silver. Since it didn't have any needle, it would be useful for giving Sam his injection.

"Now, Sam," said Lucy. "You lie down on the table."

She instructed Tommy and Betty Jean to open Sam's shirt. He was lying on the table—an old picnic table covered with a sheet—his skinny white chest facing up. "Tickle me!" he told them. "Tickle me!"

"We're not going to tickle you, Sam. We're going to do an operation." Lucy turned to Betty Jean. "The needle, please."

Betty Jean handed Lucy the hypodermic. She rolled up Sam's sleeve. Sam struggled for a moment as if his life depended on it, but Tommy and Betty Jean held him down as Lucy told them to. When Sam realized the hypodermic had no needle in it, he laughed so hard his face turned red. "Tickle me!" he said.

"OK, Sam, now this is the serious part," said Lucy. "We're about to insert the first letter of the alphabet."

For this purpose, Lucy had selected a large cake knife. It was absolutely dull, but it looked impressive. When Sam saw it, he stopped laughing.

"Now, Tommy, go get the alphabet cards from Sam's room. They're on his bookshelf. We'll hold him," said Lucy.

Tommy raced down the stairs and was back in no time. He was holding a big capital *A* up in front of Sam's eyes, and Lucy was starting to trace the very same letter on Sam's chest. She was sure this method would work, only Sam was giggling too much. The knife was tickling him. "More!" he shouted when she stopped. "Tickle me more!" Sometimes he was laughing so hard the sound stopped coming out.

"Say *A*, Sam. You've got to say *A*, or we'll have to do this letter all over again."

"*A!*" screamed Sam. "*A! A! A!*"

"Good," said Lucy. "Show him the *B*, Tommy!" Lucy drew a big *B* on Sam's chest with the cake knife.

They were just starting *X* when Mrs. Heller opened the attic door.

"Elliot!" Lucy's mother cried out. "Elliot! Where have you been all day while this was going on?"

"Paying my bills, dear," said Mr. Heller. He came upstairs and stood beside Lucy's mother. The two of them stared at Lucy and at Sam stretched out on the picnic table with his chest bared.

"I had a operation!" Sam said, pointing to his bare chest.

"Sure, Sam, sure," said his mother, picking him up and holding him as if she had just saved him from drowning. Mrs. Heller turned to Tommy and Betty Jean. She gave them a suspicious stare. "And who are you two?"

"They're Tommy and Betty Jean," Lucy tried to explain. "You know, from the new house."

"Was this your idea?" Lucy's mother glared at them.

"Oh no!" said Lucy horrified. "All mine. They were just assisting. Really." Lucy tried to smile a quick, reassuring smile at Tommy and Betty Jean. But her face felt too stiff to do it.

"Well, they'll have to go home now," said Mrs. Heller. "No more company for you, young lady!"

Tommy and Betty Jean left in a hurry. Though Lucy felt sorry for them, she felt sorrier for herself. After all, her mother had just called her a "young lady."

"This house is like a nightmare," said Lucy's mother. I come home from shopping, and when I go to put away my groceries, what do I find in the refrigerator?"

"Fish?" Lucy suggested.

"Fish!" shouted her mother. "Fish! Where did you get two hundred fish?"

"Only one hundred and forty-three, actually," said Lucy. "And I wrapped them—"

40

"Never mind! And then, I walk upstairs and I see the attic door open, and what sight greets me? This child stretched out, terrified and crying. . . ."

"He wasn't crying," Lucy explained. "He was giggling. See, I had an idea that if he could just *feel* the letters . . . and, well maybe if we frightened him *at first* so he'd pay attention . . . oh . . . and the fish were for Marmalade . . . oh . . ." and just then Lucy had too much to explain. She couldn't explain anything. Instead, she just burst into tears.

And she cried so loudly she got sent to her room. She hated to be sent to her room. But, considering the trouble she was in, it could have been worse.

"The real shame of it," said Lucy when she sat on the dock and told Marmalade all about it the next morning, "was that the operation really worked! Sam did practically the whole alphabet last night. And the best thing is that Tommy and Betty Jean convinced their mother to let them put the fish in their deep freeze. Now I can thaw some out whenever you're hungry. In fact— Marmalade! Marmalade! Where are you going? I haven't finished!"

The cat turned his head once to look at Lucy, then moved off into the woods as if he had someplace important to get to. Lucy wondered where that place was and why Marmalade had started taking his fish there.

Lucy turned around and studied the boathouse. It was painted pale orange, and the front end was clearly drooping toward the lake. It looked like a big orange cake that had fallen. The second floor, where the white railings of the dance floor were, was all boarded up.

But Lucy could imagine it fixed up beautifully— with the second floor wide open to the breeze, and strings of lights, and people dancing, and music drifting out across the lake. Then it would be quite a sight, she promised herself. Yes, if Betty Jean could see it the way Lucy saw it, even she would certainly have to admit that it was the most beautiful building on the lake.

6

Sunday Visiting

"Oh it was the most beautiful building on the lake. There's no doubt about that," said her grandfather when Lucy visited him at the nursing home the next morning. "You didn't know your grandmother. She was an unusual woman all right; she had some fantastic ideas."

"Was the dance floor her idea?"

"Oh, absolutely!" laughed her grandfather. "She wanted to give big parties. She'd invite people up from New York and have them all stay at the Star Lake Inn. And then I'd have to go over there and get them in the motorboat."

"Betty Jean—that's the girl who lives across from us—she says the motorboat is too big for the lake."

"Well, certainly. It could cross the lake in about a minute and a half," her grandfather said. "But that was the way your grandmother had to have things— on a grand scale. And she loved parties."

"I do too," said Lucy. "Don't tell Mom, but I want to give a party for her in the boathouse. And for

43

Marmalade. Because I decided Marmalade's birthday was this week. But I haven't had a chance to give him a party."

"And Marmalade would be?" It was warm today, but her grandfather had his plaid blanket across his knees as usual. He had white hair and wore those old-fashioned glasses with gold frames. Lucy liked the way he'd just sit back in his chair and let her talk to him as much as she wanted. But she didn't like the way he often forgot what she told him.

"Marmalade's my cat. Well, actually he's not really my cat, because I can't have him in the house. So he lives in the woods; I don't know where. I feed him with fish I catch, and he brings me good luck. I don't mean to brag, but guess how many fish I caught for him yesterday?"

Lucy talked and talked until her parents came back with Sam, who kept busy driving her grandfather's wheelchair. Sam had learned to set the brakes and then undo them, and he was supplying the motor sound. When it came time for her grandfather to go into the dining hall for his dinner, Sam got to push the wheelchair. Lucy would have liked to push the wheelchair herself, actually. But she had to admit Sam looked awfully interesting doing it.

When Sam pushed her grandfather into the dining room, everybody stared because you couldn't really see Sam behind the wheelchair and it looked as though the chair had pushed itself. Then Sam started bowing to everyone as if he had just given a performance. He was getting to be a ham, Lucy thought to herself. A real ham. But her grandfather's eyes were on her. After they got her grandfather settled at the table and it was time to say good-bye, he motioned to Lucy to bend down and whispered in her ear.

"Remember you were talking about Dave Seally maybe fixing the boathouse?"

Lucy nodded.

"Well, you ask him if you can see his scar."

Lucy was puzzled. Nevertheless she was always interested in looking at people's scars. So she told her grandfather she would be certain to remember. And then he started to give her a kiss. A kiss from her grandfather was always tough. His face was sandpapery, and he always kissed hard. Lucy pulled away.

"I'd rather shake hands, Grandpa."

"OK, darling," said her grandfather. He was already occupied with his soup. "See you next week. And good luck with you know what."

"What?" asked Lucy's father.

"Nothing," said Lucy.

"That's right," said Grandfather. And he held out his hand.

For Lucy to get her plans rolling meant that she had to have a talk with Dave Seally. And to do that she had to row clear across to the other side of the lake. She was glad that Betty Jean and Tommy had agreed to come with her. In fact, they were waiting for her down at the dock, with their life vests on.

Lucy's father came down to the dock to bring the rowboat around from the boathouse. "Dad," Lucy asked in a pleading voice, "could you please let Tommy and Betty Jean see the inside?" She knew that once they did, they would fall in love with it too.

When they entered, the big doors in the front were closed, and the only light inside came from the bottom of the boathouse, through the water. It was a greenish light. And when they looked down at the water, it seemed to glow. They could see the sand, and some plants, and the shadows of fish darting. No room could have had a more interesting floor.

There were spaces for two boats. The one closest was for the rowboat. And the other, deeper and wider, was for the old motorboat. The motorboat wasn't in the water, it was hanging above the water on straps.

But it was still the most beautiful boat on the lake. The seats were leather, a deep red color. And the steering wheel was brass. And the deck was mahogany, and varnished just like a dining-room table. "That's the real culprit, not the ice," Lucy's father explained to them. "That boat's what's dragging the boathouse down into the water."

Lucy knew the old boat was probably a culprit. But it had a real glass windshield with windshield wipers. And an American flag with an anchor surrounded by stars. She didn't see it as a culprit, but as a treasure. Yet she had to admit it was an awfully large treasure.

When Tommy and Betty Jean saw the motorboat,

their mouths opened. Hanging there above the water on its straps, the motorboat made the boathouse look like an eerie museum. The dark form of the old boat was lit from below by the flickering greenish light. It looked wonderful. But, Lucy supposed, if she had to choose between the whole boathouse, dance floor and all, and the motorboat, she would have chosen the boathouse.

It was a long row to the other side of the lake. Lucy got tired somewhere in the middle, and Tommy insisted on a turn at the oars. But he could never seem to keep the boat going in the same direction for very long.

Betty Jean took over. Betty Jean was skinny, but she was very strong. With Betty Jean rowing, the bow of the boat cut steadily through the water, and the little whirlpools made by the oars spun behind them. Lucy could see Dave Seally's dock getting closer. And she could see two figures, a man and a woman, walking back and forth between the house and the dock.

"There's Hilda and Dave," Lucy said.

"My mother says they're always together," said Betty Jean.

Lucy asked her what she meant by that.

"Only that she heard everyone in town has been expecting them to get married for years now. My mother thinks the reason they haven't is because Hilda's really Dave's first cousin or half sister or something."

"She's not," said Lucy.

"They could get married then," said Betty Jean. "You can't marry your brother, either, you know." She glanced at Tommy, and both she and Lucy giggled.

"I know," Lucy said. "When I was younger, I wanted to marry Sam. But then my parents told me I couldn't because the two of us were relatives by blood. I asked my mother if that means that Sam and I have the same blood. And if Sam were bleeding, could I give him some of my blood. Or vice versa." Lucy smiled. "I think it's nice to have someone you can trade blood with, even if you can't marry him."

"That's not what blood relative means," said Betty Jean. But before she could explain, Hilda was calling to them.

"What brings you three so far from home?"

"Business," Lucy shouted back.

"Oh," said Hilda.

"It's really not you we wanted to see," said Lucy when they landed their boat. "It's Dave."

"Oh, is it?" said Dave. He had just come down to the dock from the house, and he was carrying a pair of red water skis and a towrope. He was wearing a bathing suit, and so was Hilda. And he was wearing an ordinary sport shirt. It was funny for Lucy to see him without the gray work shirt that said *Dave* in script over his right pocket. And she thought of Hilda as always wearing a dress and an apron. Hilda in a bathing suit seemed like another person. She looked much younger, Lucy decided.

"Yes," said Lucy. "I mean, I *had* wanted to discuss some business with you. But I see you're going water-skiing. I wouldn't have come today except that tomorrow I have to be in school again—every day this week in fact—and it's such a long row."

"Well, since you're here," said Dave, "I'm not going to turn away any business. The economy's rather slow right now." Lucy wasn't sure she knew what the economy was. Maybe Dave would just laugh at her idea about the boathouse. She felt so uncomfortable, but why had she come all the way over here if she wasn't going to ask him?

So she plunged ahead. She told him about her plans for the boathouse and the party for her mother and Marmalade. And Dave smiled at her as though it were all some sort of cute idea a kid might have, but totally impractical. Which it probably was. Because when Lucy asked how much he would charge to do the work, Dave looked a bit embarrassed. "About a hundred years of your allowance," he answered. And then he changed the subject. "Hey! It's great that you kids showed up just now. Do you know why?"

"No, why?" said Tommy. He was a little like Sam, a little like all little kids, Lucy thought to herself in disgust. You could just change the subject and be excited about something else, and they'd forget all about what you had been talking about.

"Because," said Dave, pointing to Hilda, "this lovely young lady is going to have her first waterskiing lesson. And I have to steer the boat. We were just going to take a ride over to your side of the lake to see if we could find someone to be a spotter. Someone really reliable."

"Oh, me!" cried Tommy. He must have thought he was in school, because he was raising his hand.

"I'm older," said Betty Jean. "But I don't weigh much more than he does, so I wouldn't slow down the boat."

"What about you, Lucy?" asked Dave. "Don't you want to come?"

"I don't know if Hilda thinks I'm reliable," said Lucy.

"She is," said Hilda. "Except when she's left alone with my pies."

"Well then, pile in everyone. You'll all be spotters. I hope this is all right with you," Dave said to Hilda. And when Lucy looked, she saw Hilda smile and say "Fine." Hilda was terrific, Lucy decided. She really did like you through and through, and wasn't just pretending or just putting up with you. Lucy would like nothing better than to help Hilda learn to water-ski, even if the afternoon was a total loss from the business point of view.

7

Dave Seally's Scar

Dave's boat was probably the fastest on the lake. When she was aboard, Lucy had a chance to examine some of its peculiarities. His outboard motor had a kind of pitchfork on the bottom. That was so the propeller wouldn't get caught in weeds, he explained to Lucy.

When Hilda was all set and sitting on the dock with the skis on, Lucy stationed herself at the very rear of the boat. She wanted to see that pitchfork go through the water. Hilda, she assumed, would simply fall down. Hilda was a great baker, but Lucy had her doubts about her as a water-skier.

The pitchfork went through the water just as Lucy thought it would. Just like the fingers of a metal hand. Hilda fell eight times. And each time Dave circled around and started her again. The ninth time, Hilda actually stayed on her feet, and Dave pulled her at full speed around the lake. Lucy loved skimming over the lake. The same stretch it had taken her more than an hour to row, they crossed in minutes. She watched the wake of the boat, like a road through the water.

Hilda let go near the dock and slowed down and sank, laughing. "Oh, that was great, Dave!" she shouted, spitting out water and gasping for breath. "But that's enough. Ask the kids if they want a turn."

Betty Jean said solemnly that she knew she couldn't do it without her father's permission. And that went for Tommy, too. But Hilda had been Lucy's baby-sitter for years, and she said she knew it was all right if Lucy tried it. Soon Lucy was sitting on the edge of the dock, with the huge wooden skis floating under her like enormous feet. When the boat started to idle slowly away from her and the line got less and less tangly and started to get straight, Lucy suddenly began to feel very lonely.

Then she heard Dave roar the motor, and she felt the wooden handle she was gripping pull her off the dock. She was standing. And the water under her feet became as hard and solid as a black marble floor with flecks of white in it. The wake of the boat really was a road, and she was skimming over it so fast!

Lucy knew to keep her knees like springs, and when Dave made a turn, she let the skis run wide and cross the outside wave of the wake. Out here the water felt just a bit softer and smoother. Dave pulled Lucy in a circle around the lake. The island across from her house seemed so close when you were traveling at this speed; it didn't seem like much of a swim. In fact, the whole surface of the lake seemed no bigger than the slick floor of a room that you could slide across in your slippers.

When Lucy looked ahead at the boat, Hilda was standing up and pointing to the dock. That meant they were going in, and she should let go near the dock. When the dock seemed just the right distance, she let go of the stick, and she kept skiing for a moment toward the dock—until the water behaved like water again, and she sank into it and started to swim. She could hear cheering and clapping from the boat.

It wasn't till she was toweled off and looking at the goose bumps on her own legs that she thought again about why she had come. Lucy crouched beside Dave, who was busy stowing the towrope in the locker in the back of his boat. "Dave," she asked very sweetly, "could you do me a favor?"

"Sure, Lucy."

"Could you show me your scar?"

Dave stepped out of the boat and up onto the dock.

"Lucy Heller, what kind of a question is that?" asked Hilda. "Just because Dave was nice enough to take you waterskiing doesn't mean the poor man has to strip naked for you."

Lucy could feel herself blushing so hard the blush spread over her face like a wave of pain. Maybe

Dave's scar was in a place she couldn't look. Grandfather hadn't specified.

"When I told my grandfather I was going to ask you about fixing up the boathouse," Lucy explained, "he said to make sure I asked you to show me your scar."

Somehow, though she was telling the truth, it sounded like a complete lie. But now Dave started to grin. He was unbuttoning his shirt. And there on his stomach was a long, pale line with little pale dots on either side of it. "Those are the marks from the stitches," said Dave.

"Did my grandfather operate on you?" asked Lucy.

"He saved my life," said Dave. "And I guess this must be his way of reminding me about an old, old debt." Dave buttoned his shirt.

"You mean you never paid him?" asked Lucy. She felt bad on Grandfather's account. She wasn't sure how much an operation was worth. But if it saved Dave's life, that made it priceless. Though she wasn't sure if priceless meant worth more than anyone could count or if it meant worth nothing, at least not in money. Like water. You never paid for water, that she knew of. Yet you couldn't live without it.

"Well, at the time, I couldn't pay him," said Dave. "I was just a kid. My dad had just divorced my mom, and my brother and I had barely enough to get by on."

"Didn't you get an allowance or something? Or baby-sit?" asked Lucy.

"It would have been too much for me to pay," said Dave. "So your grandfather said I could owe it to him. But he never asked for anything. He did that with a lot of patients, or so I've heard."

Lucy had heard that, too, from her father. She had once asked him whether Grandfather had been rich. But her father had said he wasn't as rich as he could have been, because he never charged people who couldn't afford it. And around these parts, there were a lot of people like that. And they mostly came to Grandfather for treatment.

"But I guess now he wants me to pay him back," Dave went on.

"Then you'll do it?" shouted Lucy. "And it won't even be a favor will it? It will just be to repay what you owe?" This was an important point. If it were just a favor, she doubted that her father would accept the help. He didn't consider the boathouse that important anyway. To him it was just a white elephant—something big and useless—even if it was orange.

"Well, I'll *help*," said Dave. "But it's not a job I can do alone."

"My dad will help too," said Lucy. Now this might not be quite true. But she was hoping he would, especially if she tried her very best convincing on him.

"It'll take quite a few people," said Dave.

"How many is that?" asked Lucy.

57

Dave put his hand on her shoulder and crouched down so his head was level with hers. "Look, I'll tell you what. Why don't I tow you and your friends home? It's getting pretty late. And I can take another look at the boathouse while I'm there. Meantime, maybe you can think of a way of getting lots of people to help. Maybe you could make it a benefit of some sort. You know, for some good cause. A lot of people remember your grandfather around here. But I don't think you're going to see them slogging around in the mud just so you can throw a birthday party for your mom."

"You mean, if we told them it was really for the sake of a benefit, that would make a difference?" asked Lucy. It mystified her why grown-ups were willing to do some things and not others. Her mother, she decided, deserved a party at least as much as anyone. Maybe more, she thought, especially when she recalled the fish in the refrigerator yesterday.

"I'm afraid so," said Dave.

"Well, how about a benefit for orphan cats?" said Lucy. "Like my cat. He's an orphan, I think. At least he is now. He doesn't live with anyone. He just visits me and I feed him."

Dave looked doubtful again. He told Lucy to keep thinking and she might come up with something.

Meanwhile, he put a towrope around the first seat of her rowboat. Then he jumped back up onto the dock and whispered something to Hilda, who wasn't coming along. Lucy wondered if Hilda was

going to be angry that their date—if it was a date—
was being interrupted. She hoped not. After all, the
boathouse was important. Anyway, she resolved
she'd make it up to Hilda in some way. Maybe she'd
pick up all the dusty socks under Sam's bed. Or
throw out part of her dried-weed collection. She'd
think of something. But she hardly had time to think
about it now, because she and Tommy and Betty
Jean were actually going to sit in the rowboat while
Dave pulled it back to the other side of the lake.

Sam was waiting on the dock with her father when
they came around the point. Sam was in love with
motorboats. But he was afraid of their noise. He
looked like he didn't know whether to smile and
jump up and down, or hide behind her father's
pants leg.

Her father and Dave Seally talked a long time. She
could see her father walking with him up the hill
from the boathouse and then shaking his head. And
then he was nodding his head. And then he was
shaking his head again. She had no idea what, if
anything, had been agreed. Probably nothing, she
thought in despair.

Dave started up his outboard, waved to Lucy, and
drove away. And that evening, when she asked her
father what was going to happen to the boathouse,
all he said was "Lucy, don't pester me about it."

8

A Clever Idea

During recess at school, the members of the Weather Forecasters' Club were sitting around the large table in Mr. Fallsworth's room with their milk cartons in front of them. Mr. Fallsworth was explaining to them how their hair hygrometers were going to work if they built them right. "A human hair will stretch when it's damp and shrink when it's dry, and this is how we're going to tell how much water is in the air. The only problem is," said Mr. Fallsworth, "that we're going to need some very long hairs."

Mr. Fallsworth's glance moved from person to person around the table, and finally stopped at Emily Minot. Emily was the only girl in the club with very long hair, and she wore it in two long braids. Right now her arms were crossed in front of her chest, each hand gripping the end of a braid. "How about it, Emily?" said Mr. Fallsworth.

Emily didn't even smile. She just shook her head, and clenched her fists tighter.

Mr. Fallsworth opened his mouth as if to say something, but then he closed it.

Lucy was trying not to pay attention. Frankly she didn't think Emily's hair would be useful. It seemed sort of thin to her. But she concentrated on the problem at hand. If a man bought six loaves of bread for his family, and each loaf had twenty slices and cost 89¢, how many sandwiches could he make? This, she decided, was the same man who had bought all those boots a couple of pages before. Lucy was lost in a kind of daydream in which she could see the man and his wife with all those bread slices set out before them, and they were worrying if there would be enough peanut butter and jelly to put into the sandwiches—

"Lucy!" Mr. Fallsworth called over to her.

Oh no, thought Lucy. She had done it again. Much to her surprise, though, it wasn't her arithmetic homework Mr. Fallsworth wanted, but some of her hair. Lucy's hair was just as long as Emily Minot's. And Lucy knew the hairs would be even longer if she plucked them out rather than cut them. So she did—much to the amazement of the kids in the Weather Forecasters' Club. And then she went back to her arithmetic.

In a while, Mr. Fallsworth came over to see how she was doing. "You know," he said. "You could join some of the clubs if you didn't always end up having to do your homework during recess." He looked regretful, which Lucy thought was strange since it was her own fault. Perhaps he had been impressed by her plucking out the hairs. He probably thought that it had hurt. But the truth is, when your hair is very long, it's easy because you can twirl the hair around your finger three or four times so you can give it a really quick yank, and out it comes.

"That was very nice of you to give us some of your hair like that," said Mr. Fallsworth.

"Oh, think nothing of it," said Lucy. "I have plenty of hairs. I once counted four thousand eight hundred of them before my mother made me stop. I was counting out loud in the living room."

"I don't suppose it would be any use asking you why—if you can count so many hairs—you can't complete this page of simple arithmetic problems for homework," Mr. Fallsworth asked her.

"Oh, I meant to do my homework. But I had so much on my mind: fishing, my little brother's operation, Dave Seally's scar, the boathouse, my dried-weed collection, the socks under my—"

"Lucy," said Mr. Fallsworth, "you could just say 'I had many things on my mind.' "

"Sorry," said Lucy.

Mr. Fallsworth put his hands on Lucy's shoulders and looked straight at her. "The operation on your brother was nothing serious, I hope."

"Oh, yes," said Lucy. "And it was nearly a success, too. But my mother interrupted us at the letter X. I have my doubts whether Sam will ever learn Y and Z. I was so frustrated I started to cry. And then I got sent to my room."

"And what about the boathouse?" asked Mr. Fallsworth. He looked puzzled—like the man who had to make all the sandwiches.

"I decided to take your suggestion and go to speak with Dave Seally about that. And Dave said we should have some sort of benefit to fix up the boathouse. But that we should combine it with a worthy cause. Only I couldn't think of a good one until this morning when I was standing at the bus stop near my driveway, and I heard this rattling noise mixed in with a lot of squeaking noises. And that's what gave me the idea I needed. Before that, I really couldn't do my homework."

"Why not?" said Mr. Fallsworth. He seemed even more confused. Lucy hoped he wasn't about to come to the end of his patience.

"Because I was too busy thinking. However, I've finished," said Lucy. "There's something I wanted to ask you, Mr. Fallsworth, if you don't mind. In your opinion, would people be interested in a benefit to help fix up the bus that takes my brother and the other kids to the school over at Tupper Lake? Or would they be more interested in a benefit to buy our class a new globe? Somebody—probably Bobby Lattimore, but I'm not going to blame anyone for sure—put a big dent in the Pacific Ocean, pretending the globe was a soccer ball."

"I think the bus," said Mr. Fallsworth. "I think a lot of people would be interested in helping those kids. I mean the ones who are having trouble learning."

"Oh, that's Sam, all right. Sometimes it takes a real long time for him to learn something. But not always. Like yesterday, Sam said 'Throttle.' Now I know for a fact that even my mother doesn't know what a throttle is. And I think he really learned the alphabet better when we wrote it on him. I bet you didn't know everything about spelling and arithmetic when you were that age, Mr. Fallsworth, and now you're a teacher."

"You're right, Lucy," said Mr. Fallsworth. And he held her shoulder again and gave it a squeeze. She didn't know exactly why, but she didn't like where all this talk about Sam's bus had landed her. Perhaps it was the way Mr. Fallsworth had said "those kids." That was like sticking a label on Sam. But Sam was Sam. That was why she was inclined to think that the globe with the dent in the Pacific Ocean was a much safer idea for a benefit. After all, she said to herself, how are kids supposed to learn about the world if they grow up thinking it has a dent?

But everyone she talked to about it that day, even the kids, said they thought the bus was a better idea. Bobby Lattimore said his brother rode on the bus, too, and it was always breaking down. And Harold Pollard said his father had done work on the bus for the town, and it really needed a valve job, and that was expensive. And Ellen LaSalle said every time they got caught driving behind the bus it made her sick because the exhaust smelled so stinky and smoky.

So after school, Lucy convinced Tommy and Betty Jean not to go home but to stay behind with her. "You can call your mother and tell her you're walking home later. I'm sure she'll let you. And then," said Lucy, "I'll call my mom, and if she knows I'm with you two, she'll probably let me."

Lucy's mother made a big point of asking whether Betty Jean was going to be along. Her mother seemed to think sixth graders had some sort of magic quality that would protect them from accidents—which was strange. Lucy was sure she could take care of herself better than Betty Jean could.

And besides, they weren't going to go anywhere dangerous. As a matter of fact, they were just going to walk into town to the office of the *Star Lake Gazette* to get some business done. And on the way they were going to stop at Mel's Frozen Custard. "But we don't have any money," said Tommy as he scuffed along behind Lucy and Betty Jean.

"We don't need any money," said Lucy, "I have an idea."

When they arrived at the newly painted white frozen-custard stand on the main highway, Mr. Ellis —whose first name wasn't Mel—was standing in a clean white shirt and apron waiting for the first customers of the season. Just yesterday Lucy had seen him taking the plywood panels off his stand. Nobody much cared for frozen custard in the winter time.

The reopening of the stand was something Lucy always looked forward to, like the melting of the ice on the lake and her father's telling her that it would be all right to go fishing once again.

"First day of the season, huh, Mr. Ellis?" said Lucy, standing on tiptoe so she could see as much as possible, especially whether Mr. Ellis had both the chocolate and vanilla working yet. "I'll bet we're just about your first customers, aren't we?"

"That's right, Lucy. What can I offer you and your friends?"

"Oh, we can't buy anything today, Mr. Ellis. See, for the last week or so, Tommy here, and Betty Jean and I—we've been asking: Does anyone know when Mel's Frozen Custard is opening up? And nobody really did. So we're caught totally unprepared. Not like when Mel used to own the stand, of course."

Mr. Ellis was smiling at Lucy. Maybe he was remembering last summer when she'd always come up to the counter to order one cone for herself and one cone and a hundred napkins for Sam.

"I was just thinking what Mel used to do," said Lucy. "Back in the old days."

"Oh really?" said Mr. Ellis. "What did Mel do?"

"First day his stand was open in the spring, Mr. Ellis, he used to give free cones to all his customers. Then they'd go and eat the cones all over town, and it would get everyone else in the mood."

"Yes, Mel was really clever that way," said Mr. Ellis. He had already turned and begun to fill three

medium cones with a vanilla-chocolate combination. Lucy's chest felt as though it had a bird in it. Her idea was working, she thought to herself. And she took it as a good sign, since what she had to accomplish at the newspaper office seemed far more difficult. "So you knew Mel, did you?" Mr. Ellis was asking her.

"Well, not Mel, really," said Lucy. "I only heard about him. My grandfather—he's eighty-six and in a nursing home now—he used to know Mel, and my father remembers the free cones. Or I think he does. I'm pretty sure it was a true story, Mr. Ellis, only I'm just not guaranteeing it because I wouldn't want to mislead you. But you know what, Mr. Ellis?"

He had bushy white eyebrows, and he could lift them sometimes, just as he was doing now. "Your cone's going to melt if you do any more explaining," said Mr. Ellis.

"I only wanted to say that whether the story is true or not, it sure is a good idea, don't you think?"

"First-rate," said Mr. Ellis. "Now go ahead and walk all over town, and I'll wait here for the swarms of customers."

"We will," said Tommy. "We'll lick them real slowly too."

And they did. Because the cones lasted right up until the time they got to the newspaper office.

The lady sitting behind the counter typing in short, rapid explosions seemed quite severe, and she said that children were not permitted to place ads and that they were wasting her time. But then she looked up from her typewriter and wanted to know what it was the children wanted to advertise. "There's a lost-pet column, if that's what you need. And it's free, but you still have to get your parents' permission. Or are you looking for odd jobs? You look a bit young for odd jobs," said the lady.

"No," said Lucy. "It's not that at all. This is what we wanted the ad to say." She handed the lady the piece of paper she had printed so neatly during social studies:

> **Wanted.** People who owe my
> grandfather money for opera-
> tions. Our boathouse needs to
> be rebuilt. Call Lucy Heller.
> Star Lake 4372.

Lucy knew you had to make ads short. But she was quite sure she had said enough. People who had never paid for their operations would understand what she meant.

"I don't think I can run this ad without your parents' permission," said the lady. "But why don't you tell me what this is all about?"

"It's complicated," said Lucy. "See, Dave Seally is going to help us fix up our boathouse because he has a scar on his stomach from an operation my grandfather did on him that saved his life. But he says it's going to take quite a few people. So I was thinking maybe other people would like to pay my

69

grandfather back for their operations by helping out too."

"That's a clever idea," said the lady. In fact, Lucy noticed that she seemed to be thinking very hard about it. "But tell me, why is it so important to you that your boathouse be fixed up?"

"Oh, there's a million reasons for that!" Lucy answered. "For one thing, it has a dance floor on top, and we're going to have a tremendous party that's going to be a benefit. We want to charge people money for the dance and give the money to the town to fix up the blue bus that takes the kids who have to go to school over in Tupper Lake. And besides, it's my mother's birthday this month, and I think she deserves a birthday party—along with my cat, Marmalade—especially after I put all those fish in her refrigerator. But the real reason, if you want to know, is that I love that boathouse. I mean, how many boathouses have dance floors? Now that's really odd and wonderful. My grandmother thought of that."

The lady was wearing a strange sort of eyeglasses. They looked like just the bottom halves of the glasses were there and the tops had been cut off. She stared at Lucy over her glasses. Her hair was white-blond and kind of puffed up. But she didn't look really fancy to Lucy, because she had a pencil stuck in her hair. "You know," said the lady, "there might be a story here for the newspaper."

"Oh sure," said Lucy. "And you could come and

take a picture of the boathouse. Then you'd see how tilted it looks, like it's going to fall into the lake at any minute."

The lady took down all the information—even Tommy and Betty Jean's names and addresses. She thought the photograph was a wonderful idea, and she offered to drive the children home so she could be there when Sam's bus came back. Then later she wanted to talk to Lucy's mother.

9

Sinking

The newspaper lady had to talk to Lucy's mother a long time. Lucy's mother stared at the woman's camera. And then she squinted at Lucy. "What kind of thing is that to do without permission?" she asked.

"But you did give me permission," Lucy reminded her.

"To stop for ice cream," said Lucy's mother. "Not to go to the newspaper. Not to found the whole Works Progress Administration!"

Lucy didn't know what that was. But it didn't matter. Her plan was going to fail. For a while no one spoke. Lucy's mother looked at the boathouse, and then at Sam. Then her face softened.

"All *right!*" said Sam. "You're my best friend!"

"But—" said Lucy's mother, before Lucy had a chance to take even one leap or let out one whoop. "*You* don't look ready for a picture. And neither do I."

So the newspaper lady had to wait. Lucy's mother first had to fix her own hair, then Lucy's hair, and then she had to tuck in Sam's shirt. And then they stood alongside the boathouse in the sun and waited for the lady—who kept backing up to get them all in the picture—to fall off the dock.

She didn't though. And the picture was on the front page of the paper that week. Marmalade was in it. He wouldn't let Lucy hold him, but he agreed to lie on his favorite corner just as if nothing were happening. And Sam was really cute. He was holding his mother's leg and peeking out from behind it. Lucy, of course, was right in the center.

The headline went: Doctor's Granddaughter To Fix Two Ailing Relics. Headlines were short, just like ads. But there were pictures of the boathouse and of Sam's rickety old bus, too. Marmalade wasn't mentioned. But at least his picture got printed. He looked too small. But at least he was there. And Sam was mentioned—how he was driven to Tupper Lake every day with other kids from Star Lake, and how he was late sometimes because the bus broke down.

And there was even stuff about Dr. Lucius Heller, Lucy's grandfather, and all the contributions he had made to the people of the town. It was a good article. A bit boring in places, like where they said how old everyone was and what their exact addresses were and their occupations. Lucy didn't think "pupil at the Star Lake Center School" really described her. There were so many other things she did. But except for that and some other stuff, it was a pretty good article.

And the article worked, too. That Saturday there were twenty-seven people working on the boathouse. Some of the men were in the water with Lucy's father and Dave Seally, jacking the boathouse up and replacing the stone blocks underneath it. Then others began to repaint it. And later some people threw open all the plywood shutters on the top floor, cleared the old furniture out, and swept it clean.

It was an amazing sight. All at once Lucy could see right through the top of the boathouse, so that standing in her yard she could see the lake sparkling through the arched openings. But the most amazing sight was the old motorboat. Dave had it tied to the dock with his own boat on the other side of it. The American flag with the anchor was actually flapping in the wind, and the brass steering wheel was shining.

Then, too, all the beautiful wicker chairs and sofas that had been stored on the dance floor under sheets were now sitting on the lawn in the sun. Lucy had always thought of them as fat old ladies, friends of her grandmother, who had just stayed on top of the boathouse in their white dresses. But when she saw the furniture on the lawn, she decided it would look just beautiful up on top of the boathouse when there wasn't a dance there. In the warm weather, her family could sit out there, and it would be just like an open-air living room.

Lucy wanted to help with the painting. Her mother gave her an old shirt of her father's, a coffee can with a little creamy white paint in the bottom, and a small brush. Lucy enjoyed spreading the thick paint on the dirty white wood and seeing everything become new and smooth and white.

There was a tree branch that almost poked its way into the boathouse. It had gray bark. She thought maybe it would look nice painted white also. It would look just like a birch, only even whiter. She had just finished putting a first coat on the tree branch when her mother told her to stop.

It made Lucy mad that she couldn't paint anymore. After all, she was the one who had thought up this whole project in the first place. Lots of the people working there had seen her photograph in the newspaper and had told her how wonderful and clever she was. It seemed totally unfair that she couldn't paint even a single tree branch white if she wanted to.

Lucy climbed the hill in back of the house. She went up the stone steps her grandfather had built, all the way up past the terraced flower gardens that were full of colorful weeds, to the very top of the hill, where the old green water tower was. This was one of her favorite places. Up here you could hear mostly the sound of the wind blowing through the pine trees, and the voices from the house below seemed thin and remote.

Best of all, Marmalade followed her up the steps. They sat under the water tower and had a long talk. Marmalade didn't want to be near the dock just now, either. Too many people around. He and Lucy watched the people working and the cars driving up and down the driveway.

They had never seen the yard so crowded. So many voices drifted up the hill from down below. She could hear Dave Sealy giving instructions to the men and her mother shouting something to Hilda about Sam. And the air was filled with voices she didn't know. And to think, she had set all these people to work. And now she wasn't even allowed to help. She thought she should be able to paint one miserable tree branch if she wanted to.

Lucy patted Marmalade's striped, intelligent-looking face. "At least I can always count on you, Marmalade," she said. She kept stroking his fur, hard, so he could be sure to know how strongly she felt about him.

But when the cat backed away, it occurred to her that maybe he didn't like to be patted so hard—just the way she didn't like to be kissed so hard by Grandfather. "Sorry, Marmalade," she said to the cat. "I'll be gentle, gentle, gentle, with you."

"Lucy!" she could hear her mother calling. "Lucy! Where have you disappeared to?"

"That's what I've done," Lucy said softly, so that

Marmalade alone could hear. "I've disappeared, and she's not going to find me."

"Luuuucyyyyy!" her mother's voice repeated. She was shouting from the bottom of the hill, and the wind was carrying her voice high into the air, so it sounded thin and almost desperate. Suddenly Lucy felt really sorry for her mother. What if she really had disappeared? Her mother would be stuck with all that work, and Lucy wouldn't even be there to make suggestions. No, she'd have to go down, she decided. She'd have to find out what her mother wanted.

And it was a good thing she did, too. Otherwise she would have missed the most exciting event of the day. Dave Sealy had agreed to take the old motorboat back to his place to see if he could fix it up and get it running.

"And if you hurry," Lucy's mother said to her, "you and Sam can ride along in the boat."

"You mean *our* boat?" asked Lucy. This was like a dream. She and Sam were actually going to ride in it. Of course, Dave was going to tow it. The old motor wouldn't start anymore. But she and Sam could pretend the motor was working. And she could let Sam steer the boat. He'd never, never forget that. For almost a whole year now, he'd been remembering the fire engine ride he'd had on July 4th. Well, this ride would be even better than that.

When Lucy got down to the dock, Sam was already at the wheel of the old motorboat. He was wearing his orange life preserver. It looked like a fat bib. He had to stand to see through the windshield. And someone had given him a captain's hat to wear. He looked so funny, Lucy couldn't help clapping for him. He had already started to make motorboat noises.

But when Lucy got in beside him and Dave started to tow the boat out into the lake, Sam seemed to get a little scared. He sank down in his seat.

"It's all right, Sam," said Lucy. "Dave's going to tow us to his dock. You can steer all you want; it won't matter."

But it did matter. Because when Sam turned the wheel, the heavy old boat really responded. Sam could turn the boat right and left, and it followed a crazy, weaving path back and forth across the wake of Dave's boat.

"Good steering, Sam!" shouted Lucy.

It was evening now, and the lake was glassy smooth. The sun was setting, and there were streaks of red and purple over the hills in the direction they were heading. The water seemed dark and velvety, and Lucy imagined all the fish in the water going to sleep.

The way fish sleep, she told Sam, is to stay very still and all face the same direction.

"They have beds?" asked Sam.

"No, Sam. They sleep and swim slowly at the same time."

"Where are the socks?"

"No, Sam. They don't wear socks. Or pajamas either. They don't have clothes."

"No," shouted Sam. "The socks! The socks!" He seemed really mad at her all of a sudden.

"The socks!" he shouted. "Where are the socks?"

Oh, great, thought Lucy. Here I am with him, all alone in the middle of the lake, and I don't know what he's talking about, and he's ready to kill me. But then she had another thought. "You don't mean *sharks*, do you Sam?"

"Yes," said Sam, sighing with relief and exasperation.

"Oh," said Lucy. "Well then, why didn't you say so? Well, Sam, you see sharks only live in the ocean. We don't have any sharks in the lake. Just sunfish mostly."

And she began to tell him all about the fish they did have in the lake, and Sam kept driving the boat, and it was working out to be just about the most fun trip Lucy had ever had in her life, when she noticed her feet were wet.

Her feet were wet because the whole bottom of the boat was full of water. It was about bathtub depth, but it seemed to be getting deeper every second. Oh, my heavens, she thought. We're going to sink. Dave's going to turn around, and he'll just see the rope leading right down into the water, and a lot of bubbles. And Sam doesn't know how to swim.

She wondered whether she ought to mention the fact that the boat was sinking. Sam was so content, driving away, that he didn't seem to notice the deepening water under their feet. If she said something, he'd get so scared she didn't know what she'd do with him. But if she didn't signal Dave that they were leaking fast, the boat really might sink. And then what would she do with Sam?

"We have a lot of water!" she shouted to Dave. He just smiled and waved at her again. Oh, he'll be smiling and waving at us, Lucy said to herself, and we'll just sink right out of sight.

"Sam, drive straight!" Lucy said harshly. If the boat twisted on the end of the towrope, Lucy figured, it would slow them down and they might not make it.

"Okay! Okay!" said Sam apologetically. He was a good kid when the chips were down, Lucy thought to herself. But she was hoping he wouldn't notice the water, now a foot-and-a-half deep beneath them. But then, when the water reached Sam's feet on the seat, he looked down. "No water!" he shouted at Lucy. "Take away the water!"

"I can't, Sam," said Lucy. "But don't worry, you just stand up and you'll hardly get wet."

"No water!" shouted Sam. "Take it away! Take it away!"

"I can't, Sam. But we're almost at Dave's dock. Then you can get out."

"You're not my friend," said Sam.

"Oh yeah?" said Lucy. "I've let you drive the whole way. Don't I get a turn?" She figured that an argument about who got to steer might make him forget that the boat was sinking. "And anyway, what's wrong with a little water? You won't get too wet. Here. Stand on this cushion."

Lucy put a boat cushion under Sam's feet, and it raised him just enough to keep him out of the water. I hope we get there soon, she said to herself. Her legs were wet, and she was starting to get cold.

The boat didn't sink until it was a few feet away from the dock. Hilda was standing there, and she grabbed Sam before he got too scared or wet. Dave stared as if he couldn't believe what he was seeing. The boat sank lower and lower, until only the windshield and the American flag with the anchor were showing. Then they went under. And much to Lucy's surprise, there weren't even any bubbles.

"For heaven's sake," said Dave. "It could have sunk with you in it. Why didn't you signal me?" He looked at Lucy as if she had done something very strange.

"I did signal you," said Lucy. "Quietly, of course. I didn't want to panic Sam. And you smiled at me and waved. So I figured you couldn't be too worried. I guessed you were sure we'd make it."

"She was scared, Dave," said Hilda. "You can't blame her, only yourself. Didn't you know the boat was leaky?"

By this time Lucy was crying, and Hilda was holding her.

"I was scared for Sam," she said. "I can swim for miles. But I knew he'd go crazy in the water. And *then* what was I going to do?"

"OK, OK," said Dave. "You did the right thing. You really did." And then he looked at the dark, featureless water where the boat had been just a few minutes ago. "I suppose you did the right thing. Boy, I'd never have thought the boat was that leaky!"

Then he and Hilda and Lucy all started to laugh at once. And Sam too started to scream with laughter, though he didn't seem quite sure what the joke was. "Leaky boat!" he shouted. "Leaky boat!"

Later that evening, after Sam was in bed, Lucy came down to the dock, in the dark, to leave a fish for Marmalade. She'd had quite an adventure she wanted to tell him about.

As she stood there, the boathouse looked strange to her. The railings up above were glowing brightly with their new coat of white paint. "Marmalade!" she called. "Oh, Marmalade! Supper!" Lucy stood there on the dock a long time. She kept listening as hard as she could to hear the sound of the cat rus-

tling through the bushes. But she didn't hear anything except the waves lapping up against the dock.
She wondered if perhaps all those people today had
frightened him away. She left the fish on the dock
and started back toward the house.

10

Did Helen of Troy Have Freckles?

"So you see," she explained to her grandfather when she was visiting him the next morning at the nursing home, "we did have a few problems. Just because I painted the tree a little bit white, Mom told me I couldn't help anymore. And fixing up the boathouse was my idea! And then the motorboat sank, and I got really scared for Sam. Though it was funny too, I guess. And then, when I wanted to tell Marmalade about it, he wouldn't come down to the dock for his dinner."

"Who's Marmalade?" asked her grandfather.

"I told you last week," said Lucy. "And I told you the week before that, too." Sometimes she had the feeling her grandfather forgot everything she said to him. So what was the point of talking to him?

"Tell me again, darling."

"He's my cat," said Lucy a bit grudgingly.

"He's a male?" asked her grandfather. She had told him all that before. And what color Marmalade was. But she might as well run through the whole thing again. Very old people sure forget things fast, she said to herself. As for herself, she had a good memory. And she would never, ever be that forgetful. Especially about Marmalade.

"Well, if he's a male, he'll wander off from time to time. Male cats like adventure," said her grandfather. "But he'll be back. If you were kind to him and if you fed him, he'll be back."

Lucy told her grandfather about the hundred and forty-three sunfish she had caught for Marmalade. Of course, she had told him before. But he didn't remember, so he enjoyed the story all over again.

And when she had finished telling him about that, she told him about the party. And the green crêpe dress her mother was going to wear. And how many people had bought tickets already. And how much money they were going to raise to fix up Sam's bus. She was surprised when her mother told her it was time for her grandfather's dinner. Some visits with him passed really slowly, but not this one.

"Do I get a handshake or a kiss this time?" asked her grandfather. His blue eyes looked hard at her from behind the gold-rimmed glasses he wore.

"A kiss," said Lucy. He sure remembered that, Lucy thought to herself. Maybe he just pretended to forget, so she could tell him the same things all over again. This kiss was about as rough as usual. But worth it, Lucy decided.

That afternoon, Tommy and Betty Jean came over, and they climbed the hill in back of Lucy's house, all the way up to the water tower. From this height, they could look down on the boathouse. It seemed especially orange with its new coat of paint. Lucy invited Tommy and Betty Jean to come to the party. "It's going to be great. There'll be music and dancing, and my mom's going to wear her green crêpe dress."

"I don't like dancing," said Tommy. "And I'll bet there'll be a lot of kissing, too."

Lucy was just about to ask Tommy why he thought there'd be a lot of kissing when she heard a crash in the woods. She saw Marmalade streak by, running for his life. Duke came next, and right where the children were standing, he made a skidding turn. Tommy and Betty Jean screamed at Duke to stop, but he didn't listen to them. Lucy knew Marmalade could climb a tree. But why *hadn't* Marmalade climbed a tree? And just as she was thinking that, she saw it.

It was running also, like a bright streak through the woods. At first she thought it was a rabbit and that Duke and Marmalade were having a race to see who could catch it. But then, it darted away from Marmalade, and Lucy could see it was a white cat. It climbed a tree, and Marmalade kept running and climbed another tree farther off. Duke, confused, sniffed a few times at the base of the first tree, then left it to sniff at the base of Marmalade's tree, then came back to the tree where the white cat sat on a high branch.

It looked just like the white cat Lucy had dreamed about. The opposite of Marmalade's shadow. Perhaps Marmalade had climbed a different tree to give the white cat more time to escape? Oh, Marmalade, you're the best cat that was ever born, Lucy thought to herself. And then she wondered if the white cat was owned by anyone. "Come visit us," shouted Lucy. "We're having a party for Marmalade!" The cat turned its head and glanced at her from high in its tree.

"He'll keep them there all day," said Tommy. He and Betty Jean tried calling to Duke. Duke kept running from tree to tree and barking while the two cats sat on their high branches and watched him.

When Duke finally quit, he looked tired and as dumb as ever. He had burrs in his fur, and his tongue was hanging out, which Lucy knew was the way dogs sweat. She didn't want to get into a fight with Tommy or Betty Jean, but in her opinion that dog really was a fool.

Marmalade and the white cat both stayed in their trees till the children couldn't stay outside anymore. Lucy wasn't sure when they came down or where they went. But they were both good climbers, she told herself, and there were plenty of trees around if Duke should try to chase them again.

The next day, when Lucy came home from school, the screened porch looked like a bakery shop. Hilda had made pies and cookies and pastries, and had set them all out to cool. After school she offered Lucy and Sam their first choice of cookies. Then their second choice.

All week long, Hilda was humming in the kitchen, and on Thursday, when Mrs. Heller got home, she and Hilda even tried on their dresses for each other.

Lucy came into her mother's bedroom to watch. "Oh Hilda," Lucy's mother was saying, "you look so lovely! If that Dave Seally had any sense—" She kept looking at Hilda, shaking her head and smiling. "Well, he probably just needs a little push." And then Hilda and her mother burst out laughing.

Lucy paid no attention to this silliness. She was trying to decide which dress she thought was prettier. Of course, her mother's green crêpe dress was Lucy's favorite, but Hilda's dress was really beautiful too. It had big red flowers that looked like poppies magnified a thousand times and long spearlike green leaves. When Lucy stared at the dress, she felt the way a bee might feel when it was about to land on a flower.

The big question for Lucy, however, was not what she was going to wear for the party, but what to get her mother and Marmalade for presents. She decided her mother would definitely be thrilled with the Leaning Tower of Pisa. It had started out as a cream pitcher in art class, but had developed a tilt that Lucy couldn't fix. Maybe some of the other kids would have mashed it, but Lucy punched some holes in it for windows and decided it made an excellent replica of the Leaning Tower. If you squinted a bit.

Marmalade's gift presented another problem entirely. Lucy tried to think about what she knew of his likes and dislikes. OK, she said to herself. Marmalade definitely dislikes dogs, so I won't give him a present that has anything to do with dogs. But Lucy couldn't think of what Marmalade *would* like. Marmalade was a boy cat. So she decided to ask Sam. Maybe he could think of something.

Sam was busy in his room, playing his rhythm instruments. He was banging his cymbals so hard Lucy didn't think he noticed her. But he did, because he handed her a pair of maracas. They made a lot of noise together for a while, and then Lucy asked him to stop.

"I've got something serious to ask you about, Sam, and you've got to listen hard," she said to him firmly. Then she took his cymbals away from him so he had to listen. "I want to give a nice present to Marmalade, but I'm not sure what to give him. Now, he's a boy cat, so I thought I'd ask you for ideas. If you were a cat, Sam, what sort of present would you like?"

Sam got up off the floor and came back with his raggedy blanket. "I'm going to sleep with Curly."

"Are you suggesting that we give him Curly?" asked Lucy in disbelief. "You'd really do that, Sam?" She tried to yank Curly out of Sam's arms. "Oh, thank you, Sam. But I don't know if I can really accept such a generous offer, even for Marmalade."

Sam kept a tight grip on his blanket, and Lucy kept pulling. Finally Sam was doubled over with laughter, and all he could say was "No, Lucy, no!" as Lucy dragged him over the slippery floor of his room using the blanket as a towrope. "Well, thank you for the offer, Sam. But really, Curly is so ratty-looking, I think I'd better find Marmalade a cleaner blanket. Thanks anyway, Sam!" And she left him right where he was on the floor.

But of course Sam *had* given her a wonderful idea. There were some other flannel blankets just like Sam's in the linen closet, and she knew of a basket in the attic she could use to make Marmalade's bed. She spent the whole evening weaving Marmalade's new bed with ribbons, lining it with flannel, and then wrapping it in yards of wrapping paper and ribbon until the job was done perfectly.

If Lucy could have had her way, they'd have canceled school that Friday since it was the day before the party. Even more than usual, she had trouble keeping her mind on her arithmetic problems. The man who'd bought the six loaves of bread had now gone shopping for twenty bottles of hair tonic. What would he do with them? This made her wonder if Dave Seally would be wearing hair tonic when he got dressed up for the party, and if Hilda's new dress would enchant Dave, and if Marmalade would really love his new bed and climb right in it first thing and go to sleep.

At lunchtime, as Lucy was completing her unfinished arithmetic, Mr. Fallsworth was holding a meeting of the Greek Mythology Club. The Greek Mythology Club was having an argument about who should play the part of Helen of Troy. She was a queen who lived a long time ago in ancient Greece, Mr. Fallsworth had told them. Everyone started to tease Emily and say she should play Helen of Troy. For a costume, she could wear a bed sheet. "The face that launched a thousand ships!" said Mr. Fallsworth. He meant that Helen had been so pretty, a whole army—a thousand ships full of men—had gone after her when she had run away.

To Lucy, trying to concentrate on her arithmetic, the whole story seemed quite silly. She couldn't imagine people fighting a whole war over just one person, especially a girl as silly as Emily wrapped up in a bed sheet.

She tried to force herself to think about the problem in front of her. "If hair tonic costs 97¢ a bottle, and each bottle holds 6½ ounces, and half the bottles are made of plastic, how much would twenty bottles cost?"

There they go again, thought Lucy. She would even have preferred to join the Greek Mythology Club. She walked over to the table where the club was meeting.

"I could play Helen of Troy," said Lucy.

"No you couldn't," said Emily. "Because you aren't a member of the club. You're supposed to be doing your arithmetic homework. And anyway, you

92

have freckles. And Helen of Troy didn't have freckles."

The members of the Greek Mythology Club all started to talk at once. They were arguing over whether Helen of Troy could have had freckles. Mr. Fallsworth explained to them that there were no pictures of Helen. Though some Greek statues existed from thousands of years ago. Mr. Fallsworth was probably right. She had started flipping through the thick book, called Homer's *Iliad,* which told the story of the Trojan War. And the only picture of Helen was a statue of a woman wearing practically nothing, and the statue had its arms knocked off.

"Well maybe the statues had freckles painted on them, and they faded?" said Lucy. Emily really got on her nerves. She just wanted to play Helen because Bobby Lattimore was going to play Paris, the man Helen ran away with.

"You know, Lucy," said Mr. Fallsworth, "I've told you many times that if you would like to join some of our clubs, we'd love to have you. But only if you have your homework done. I'm not even going to ask you why it wasn't done for today. Why, even if you had a whole weekend, you wouldn't spare a few moments to do your homework."

"OK, Mr. Fallsworth," said Lucy. "I won't even try to explain."

The room became very quiet. The members of the Greek Mythology Club had stopped bickering.

They were waiting to see if Mr. Fallsworth would ask Lucy what her excuse was. But Mr. Fallsworth seemed to have closed his eyes for the moment. He seemed to be counting to a hundred in his head. "All right," he finally said very softly. "I can't resist. I have to hear the story. I have a feeling it's going to be more complicated than the story of Helen of Troy."

"Oh no," said Lucy. "It's very simple. I was making a bed for Marmalade, my cat."

"That's all?" asked Mr. Fallsworth. "Are you sure it isn't some complicated excuse? Something to do with the party tomorrow?" He sounded almost disappointed.

"This book here, Mr. Fallsworth," said Lucy, "Homer's *Iliad*? Is that the story of Helen of Troy?"

"Yes," said Mr. Fallsworth. "One of the world's first great stories."

"But it has some real boring parts, doesn't it?" Lucy turned back to the page she had just glanced at, and started to read it to the class:

> . . . and the goddesses gathered about her,
> all who along the depth of the sea were daughters
>   of Nereus.
> For Glauke was there, Kymodoke and Thaleia,
> Nesaie and Speio and Thoë, and ox-eyed
>   Halia . . .
> Doto and Proto, Dynamene and Pherousa,
> Dexamene and Amphinome and Kallianeira;
> Doris and Panope and glorious Galateia. . . .

And then it went on even more. When Lucy was finished, nobody said anything.

"Mr. Fallsworth," said Lucy. "Isn't that a rather long list?"

"Yes, Lucy, it is," said Mr. Fallsworth.

"And Homer's *Iliad* is one of the first great stories?"

"Yes, Lucy," said Mr. Fallsworth. He seemed to sigh.

"Well, good!" said Lucy. "In that case, Mr. Fallsworth, would you like to hear who's coming to the party tomorrow? Or would it be better if I started with a list of what we're having to eat?"

11
Flying

The party was turning out to be the best one ever held in Star Lake. Mr. Bartlett agreed to take people for sunset rides in his seaplane, and the money he collected was turned over to the fund for Sam's bus. Early that evening, when the first guests were arriving, the bright green airplane was anchored not far from Lucy's dock. Then Mr. Bartlett slipped the anchor and started the engine with an incredible roar. And the plane coasted out toward the open lake, picking up speed until it flew off into the air.

Each time it took off, people came down onto the dock to watch and applauded. Dave Seally came down with Hilda. They were going to be the next to ride. Three could go at one time, and Dave asked Lucy if she'd like to go. "After all," he said "you were the mastermind of this whole business."

Lucy liked that. *Mastermind.* Of course. But still it was nice when someone remembered. She ran to ask her parents' permission. They were standing in front of the boathouse, all dressed up.

Just as her mother seemed about to say no, her father said it might be all right. "I'm sure it's safe, Nora," he said to Lucy's mother. "And besides, Lucy deserves the reward. After all, the whole party was her idea in the first place."

What was getting into people? thought Lucy. Everybody was appreciating her, for once! She was beginning to feel famous or something. The seaplane was landing out in the middle of the lake, and now it was turning toward the dock. Lucy ran down to join Dave and Hilda. When the plane pulled closer, it suddenly looked much, much larger to Lucy than it ever had. She was used to seeing it on the other side of the lake, and from that distance, it looked like a toy.

The long green wing seemed to cast a very dark shadow on the water when Lucy stepped aboard. She was wondering who would get to sit in front with Mr. Bartlett. She thought maybe Dave would, since he had the longest legs. But he wanted to sit in back with Hilda, he said. So Lucy got to sit in front. Her seat had a steering wheel in front of it, just like Mr. Bartlett's. She hoped she wouldn't be expected to steer. The cabin was small and complicated. There were at least forty dials right in front of her.

When Mr. Bartlett started up the motor, the propeller made its own windstorm on the lake. Then the seaplane began to drift forward, and soon it was skimming the water as fast as Dave's boat could, maybe faster. Yes, definitely faster. Before Lucy was quite ready for it, the surface of the lake was dropping away, and they were in the air.

Mr. Bartlett had to shout to be heard. But he pointed out her window and told her to look down. And there, sure enough, was her house, the boathouse, the driveway with its little white squares of marble in a neat pattern, the sandbar, the water tower, all her favorite places. But from up here, she could see that it was only a small, small part of the land around the lake. Beneath her she could see green hills, with other lakes shining between them.

The ride was bumpier than she had thought it would be. Mr. Bartlett's plane seemed to sway and bounce, almost as a boat does when the water is choppy. The air felt solid up here, like something hard and rough. Dave and Hilda were squeezed into the small backseat of the plane. Dave had his arm around Hilda, and Lucy wondered if that was to save space or if he just enjoyed sitting that way.

When Mr. Bartlett flew low over her house, Lucy could see her parents and Sam standing on the dock. Sam looked so small, like a little blond dot between her parents. But she could see he was pointing up at her. Lucy wished she knew what he was saying. He was waving to her. Lucy waved back, though she doubted he could see her.

"Do you want to go down now?" Mr. Bartlett was

shouting at her. "You look a little green." Lucy felt a little green. She never got seasick in the rowboat, even in the roughest of storms, but this plane was rougher. Maybe when they landed, Mr. Bartlett would let Sam sit in the airplane and pretend he was driving it. He'd probably prefer that to a real ride, she thought to herself.

Lucy was most excited by the landing. The plane circled the lake and then seemed to follow a down-hill path toward the water. It bounced a few times when it touched the water, and then the engine was louder than ever, almost as though the plane were angry that it had to stop flying. But Lucy was glad to be down. Being up in the air was OK, but she could see more and more cars parking in their long driveway, and she was eager to get down to the boathouse again to see if the band had arrived and if people were dancing.

Her mother hugged her at the dock, as though she had been away for weeks, and Sam was full of questions: "Where did you fly? What did you do? Who drives that?" But Lucy broke loose from them. She wanted to go up to the boathouse. She could hear soft music playing, and at the railings overlook-ing the lake, guests were standing with champagne glasses in their hands, talking or gazing at the sun-set. It looked just the way she had dreamed it would.

When Lucy reached the second floor of the boat-house, everyone was dancing. Lucy always liked to watch people shaking and swaying and gliding. Everyone did it differently. And sometimes the fattest people were the most graceful, like Bobby Lattimore's parents. But suddenly the musicians stopped playing. And as if someone had called out "Freeze!" all the grown-ups were still, and they were looking at her.

"To Lucy Mastermind," the band leader called out, and Lucy realized he was talking about her. Well, Sam could show off at the nursing home. So she didn't suppose there was any harm. She walked right down the center of the room.

It was like walking through a forest of people. When she got in front of the band, she took one of those theatrical bows. There was a roar of clapping.

"I'm going to try some of the punch," Lucy said.

And that pleased everyone too. Lucy had an idea that anything she said would be a hit, all because they were having such a good time.

But the best part was when the men who had gone to get her grandfather from the nursing home carried him up the stairs in his wheelchair, so he could see everything. After all, it was his boathouse. Lucy ran to give her grandfather a hug, and she could see he looked sort of dazzled.

People kept coming up to her grandfather, leaning down to him, and shouting their names. Maybe they thought he was deaf, just because he was old. But he could hear them.

Bobby Lattimore's father was talking to Grandfather. "You took care of me when I was a kid," he was saying.

"Sure, I remember you," said Grandfather. "You've gotten overweight." Her grandfather sounded grouchy, but Lucy could see that he really wasn't. His eyes looked lively. And he seemed amused by something, almost as though he thought the party was silly. But Lucy could see it was making him happy anyway.

"Well, you've got some granddaughter," said Mr. Fallsworth. He had come over to Lucy's grandfather and was leaning over his chair. "She's in my class. And let me tell you, she's got more ideas in that head of hers. . . ."

Lucy's grandfather slowly shook Mr. Fallsworth's hand. Then he turned to look at Lucy. "She takes after my wife," he said in a voice that was softer than usual. Lucy didn't know. She'd never met her grandmother, though she'd often thought they'd have enjoyed thinking up things to do together. But what her grandfather said made her feel proud. The sensible thing, she decided, was to turn some cartwheels.

She did a few cartwheels right down the dance floor. And, as usual, she did them so quickly her underpants didn't show. It was fun watching the whole party—all the ladies in their bright spring dresses and the men in their tan, and brown, and dark gray suits—flip over a few times.

"Lucy," she could hear her mother saying very sternly. But Lucy didn't stop for any more applause. She was already down the steps and running across the lawn and into the darkness, leaving the boathouse, with its light and noise, behind.

12

Marmalade

Lucy peered into the woods and called "Marmalade! Marmalade!" Maybe the cat was upset by all the lights and music and wouldn't come near her. She tried to see if his eyes were shining from behind a bush, but she couldn't tell. She checked in back of the garage, and then crossed the driveway and started to climb the stone steps up the hill to the water tower. It was getting very dark now, but she knew that Marmalade would be able to see her. That is, if he were around. But was he?

She tried to think how many days it had been since she had actually seen Marmalade. Yes, it had been the day after Duke had chased Marmalade and the white cat. Since then, she had been putting his fish out on the dock as usual. But perhaps some other animal had been taking them.

Now it came down on her like a heavy weight. Marmalade had probably run away. Or someone had kidnapped him and put a collar on him and was his owner. She felt as though she were in a big hole, and people were dumping sand on her chest. It was hard to breathe. "Oh, Marmalade," she cried. "Where are you?" She yelled as loud as she could, and then listened for a meow.

But all she could hear was the music and people laughing. What was so funny? Grown-ups could see each other, then they'd scream some sort of loud "Hello, I haven't seen you in ages!" and then they'd hoot with laughter. Listening to it from up here in the woods, it seemed ridiculous.

Yet this was the party she had wanted so much. Why didn't Marmalade show up? she thought angrily. He was too independent, that was his trouble. "Stupid cat!" she shouted into the darkness. "Don't come down. I'm not going to give you your new bed. I'm through with you, Marmalade!" Lucy shouted in her anger. "Don't even bother coming down now!" Lucy listened for a moment. The wind blew through the trees and made the pine branches whoosh. The music started playing down in the boathouse. Lucy thought she could hear her mother's laughter amidst the crowd of voices. And this made her feel even more alone.

It was her father who found her near the steps to the boathouse. He'd been looking all over for her. She wasn't used to seeing him in a tie. And he smelled nice, too, as though he had been using some of that cologne in the football-shaped bottle that she and Sam liked to experiment with. "That smell reminds me of when Sam used to wear diapers," she said to him when he sat down next to her on the boathouse steps.

"That bad, huh?" said her father.

"No. I just mean that it reminds me of the day I poured cologne on Sam's diapers. Remember? My idea was that that way we'd only have to change him once a day."

"Yes," said her father.

"Not one of my better ideas," said Lucy.

"Well, you were little then," said her father. "But this party," he said, pointing in back of them to where the bright lights of the boathouse were shining out onto the lake, "was definitely one of your better ideas."

"Yes," said Lucy.

"Then, why have you been crying? Can't think up anything to do next? All schemed out?"

"Marmalade's gone," said Lucy.

"Oh," said her father.

"Daddy!" shouted Lucy. "It's been since Monday!"

"Oh," said her father very softly. "I see. That's a long time. And you're frightened that he's run away?"

"Or that he's gone to live with someone else."

"Well he couldn't be so stupid to go live with anyone else. Who else would feed him real fish every day?"

Just the way her father was trying to make her feel better made everything worse than before.

"Look," said her father, "maybe you're overexcited and tired out. I'll tell you what. I'll help you get ready for bed. And when you're all ready for bed, I'll tell you some very, very good news."

"I don't want to hear any news," said Lucy. "Except the news that Marmalade's come back."

"Well some of this news *is* about Marmalade. C'mon," said her father, and he put his arm around her. She did feel tired, she had to admit.

When she was all ready for bed and had pulled her quilt up under her chin, her father sat down beside her to kiss her good-night. He was so heavy, he tilted the bed. "What's the good news?" she asked.

"Three things, really," said her father. "The first is that we raised enough money from the party, counting the money from the seaplane rides, so that the bus can be fixed."

"I could have told you that," said Lucy. But she couldn't help smiling a little.

"And the second piece of good news is that it isn't going to be Sam's bus anymore. His teacher came tonight and happened to mention that she's going to recommend that Sam attend kindergarten at your school next year. So he can ride to school on the same bus with you."

"Now that's *wonderful* news," said Lucy. "Sam will

look so cute getting on the bus with all the bigger kids, and if any of the kids start up with him, they'll have to watch out for Tommy, Betty Jean, and me."

"Who would start up?" asked her father.

"Well, you never can tell," said Lucy. "Next fall we might have some new enemies."

"Next fall is a long time away," said her father, switching off the light. "There's a whole summer to be gotten through first."

"Right," said Lucy. "Now tell me about Marmalade."

"Well," said her father. "Now that the boathouse is fixed, your mother and I figured a cat ought to live in it. To keep the mice away, and so on. But you really, really must promise not to let Marmalade in the house. If it's very cold, we can plug in an old heating pad out there. Of course, you can have a name tag made that says MARMALADE, with your name and address on it too. Buy him a catnip mouse if you want. And a personalized bowl. Get him shots at the veterinarian's. Claw clippers. Flea collar. The whole disagreeable works." The more her father spoke of it, the gloomier he sounded. But to Lucy, it was as if an enormous door had been thrown open. Before her father had even finished, Lucy was out of bed hugging him.

He said good-night, but now Lucy was too excited to go to sleep. Maybe Marmalade *would* come back. Especially now that he could really belong to her. And as she closed her eyes, she could hear the music from the party, and grown-ups laughing way too loud, and cars starting to go home.

And she even dreamed that she heard meowing, lots of meowing. She was just starting to dream about getting onto the bus with Sam next year, with her arm around him and all the other kids envying her because she had such a cute little brother, when she sat up straight in bed. Those meows were no dream. Those were real meows, only there were also some tiny high sounds. Almost as though a cat had caught some mice, and the mice were meowing too, trying to plead with the cat to let them go.

Lucy tried to figure out where the sound was coming from. As best she could tell, it was from below the window in her parents' room, on the other side of the house. But when she looked out the window, she couldn't see anything except the lawn, dark and empty. Yet the sound was definitely closer. Lucy crept down the stairs, listening the whole time, and made her way through the living room, out onto the sun porch. Now the sounds were very close. *Meow. Meow.* And that meow sounded like Marmalade's. Lucy would have known it anywhere. But what was Marmalade doing so close to the house? He never came up this close.

Very quietly she opened the porch door and walked outside. The grass was cold and wet under her bare feet. She went around to the back of the house, the side that faced the lake, and it was very dark there. But the sound was closer. It seemed to be coming from the pit in front of the basement window. When Lucy peered into the pit she saw something that nearly made her heart stop. It was the white cat, sleeping on a bed made from grass and an old towel. And nestled around her were four tiny, tiny kittens.

Just then Marmalade came toward her from the shadows under the trees. He brushed against her leg and pushed his head up against her hand when she patted him. Then he stood at the edge of the pit and sniffed toward the white cat and the tiny kittens. The white cat lifted her head nervously, but Marmalade stayed back and was very cautious and gentle.

"Those are your kittens too, aren't they, Marmalade?" Only a dim light from the porch was shining down into the pit, but Lucy thought she could make out Marmalade's orange coloring on two of the kittens. One was pure white, like the mother. And one had patches of each color, as though parts of the white cat and parts of Marmalade had been put into a bowl like cake ingredients and mixed together.

"You brought them here so they would be safe, didn't you? You brought them home to us." She circled her arms around Marmalade and gave him a quick, gentle hug. Marmalade didn't like to be hugged hard, but Lucy just had to hug him a little. "You're a good cat, Marmalade. The best cat in the whole wide world."

"Imagine a cat bringing along his wife and family," said Mr. Heller. "Now that I've never heard of." He was standing in front of the boathouse, saying good-bye to some of the guests. He seemed amazed, but not exactly pleased. "And to think: Here I am allergic to cats, and now we have . . . How many did you say there were, Lucy?"

"Six," said Lucy. "Marmalade, and the white cat, and four kittens. One plus one equals six, Dad. Funny, that's what I once imagined Marmalade telling me. I guess it's his sort of arithmetic."

"I wish he had told me," said Mr. Heller. "I would have found a home for him and his family somewhere near Tupper Lake."

"Daddy! You promised me I could have a cat," said Lucy. "And Marmalade's my cat. He's married. And he and his wife have four children. Now that means they are all our cats, right? How would you like it if someone divided us up, and Sam had to go live over at Tupper Lake, and Mom went to New York, and I lived in Istanbul or somewhere, and you were left here all by yourself? How would you feel? Marmalade loves his family, and he's a good father. I'd think you of all people would understand that!"

"Lucy," said Mr. Heller, "sometimes I honestly wonder where you come from. I don't think we've ever had such a good arguer in the family."

"Yes we have," said Lucy. "Grandma! After all, look at that." Lucy pointed to the boathouse that was still all lit up, and it did look like something out of another country or a dream. When Grandmother

112

first thought of it, it must have seemed like such an unusual idea. But she must have talked Grandfather, the carpenters, the bricklayers, everyone, into believing it could be done.

"I've got to tell Mom. And I've got to tell Hilda and Dave. And I've got to tell the lady from the newspaper. I've got to tell Mr. Fallsworth. I've got to tell everybody. See you later, Dad." Lucy left him standing there, about to say something, but she didn't have time to wait around.

The lady from the newspaper said, "That's almost like a miracle. Cats never do that. It's like a reward to you for thinking up the idea for this generous benefit."

Her mother said, "Oh no. Now there'll be fish in the refrigerator forever."

And Mr. Fallsworth said, "Four kittens? *You* won't pick ordinary names, will you? Lucy! I have an idea! Why don't you use some of those names from Homer's *Iliad*? Halia, Dexamene, Galateia—"

"Oh, I don't know," said Lucy. "I was thinking of something simpler, like Henry maybe?"

"Henry?"

"Yes," said Lucy. "Isn't that right?"

Mr. Fallsworth turned red, just the way he did when he was angry, but he was smiling. He started to say something about how fascinating it was to watch how a litter of kittens developed, but Lucy couldn't wait around. She wanted to find Dave and Hilda and tell them the good news.

When she found them, though, she decided not to

interrupt them. They were sitting in the old green rowboat, kissing. Lucy noticed the oars leaning against the wall of the boathouse. She smiled to herself and, without saying anything, untied the boat and gave it a gentle shove, so that it started to drift away from shore. Hadn't her mother said Dave just needed a little push?

It was very late when Lucy got back into bed, but she had a lot of trouble falling asleep. She kept listening for the sound of the cats near the basement window. And she also heard more cars starting up and the last of the guests leaving. And then she heard Dave's voice shouting "Hey! Someone come out here!" And that sound seemed to be coming from the middle of the lake.

She hoped her little push had worked. Then maybe there could be another party in the boathouse. Perhaps a small wedding. Well, at least Dave had stopped shouting. And now, lying in bed, Lucy could hear only the wind stirring the branches of the trees outside her window. But even this sound had something interesting in it, or something she hadn't heard in a while, anyway.

It was the rustling of leaves. Lucy took a deep breath. Yes, she could almost smell summer on its way. Soon there wouldn't be any more arithmetic. And she and Sam could spend all their time watching the kittens grow, and she could even get started on her next project: teaching Sam to swim out to the

114

sandbar. It was true, he was still afraid to put his face in the water. But so what? Of course, she could also build a tree house or tame a pet spider with hamburger. . . . Oh, she had a long list. But summer lasted a long time. And if she knew anything at all, she knew that the things she set her mind to usually happened.

ALAN FELDMAN says, "This book is based on a fusion of my childhood with my daughter's. I once lived in the house Lucy lives in, and it was just the sort of house my daughter would have loved. By writing *Lucy Mastermind,* I let her occupy it. My idea for the book also comes from our family life now: Sam has much in common with my son. And I can see that this book—about mischief, but also about kindness —is a record of the relationship between my two children."

Mr. Feldman, a poet whose work has appeared in *The Alantic* and *The New Yorker,* won the Elliston Book Award with his first book of poems, *The Happy Genius.* He lives in Framingham, Massachusetts, where he is professor of English at Framingham State College.

IRENE TRIVAS has illustrated numerous books, including the Robot series by Ann Cook and Herb Mack, *The Pain and The Great One* by Judy Blume, and *Snip* by Nathaniel Benchley. She lives in South Ryegate, Vermont.